Bonne Chance &
Butterflies

Rosie Christopherson   2019

For Suzi
Follow your dreams
warm hugs
love
Rosie

Heartfelt thanks to Huw my partner for his unwavering support, technological expertise and encouragement, to Keith Dixon for sharing his literary knowledge which enabled me to make a start, to Mike Evans, and the many dear friends, who are so much a part of my life in this magical town.

"We can't go back to the start to change the beginning, but we can start now to change the end."
C.S. Lewis

Montmorillon is a real town in Nouvelle Aquitaine, rural France. Set against the back drop of the medieval Cité de L'Ecrit, city of writing. Events and Izzy's character are fictional, though the places and some of the characters are real.

Chapter 1

Harriet's turquoise coffin added a glow to the Park Orchards Baptist Hall.

It looked strangely out of place perched on the austere trolley. Bowls of white roses provided by the ladies committee trying hard to soften their stark surroundings. Jesus on a wooden cross staring down at the rows of numb bottom seating.

The only warmth in this room lapping in the baptismal, concealed below a sliding floor, heated to a constant 20 degrees ready to wash away the sins of the next convert.

The church committee voted two years ago not to go ahead with a plan for central heating, persisting with three tiny wall heaters. "The money is better spent on the missions," declared Pastor Jean. Nobody brave enough to vote against her. It certainly stopped people falling asleep, it was just my luck that Harriet died in the winter.

Australia conjures up visions of sand and sea, but it's bloody freezing in a wintery Melbourne. Harriet is cosy in her coffin, wrapped in her jade suede jacket and tartan skirt. Wearing my snug sheepskin boots and floor length burnt orange coat, I am determined to match warmth with colour. Bricks, mortar and no windows make this Baptist hall more like a soulless prison cell than a place of worship.

Double entrance doors provide the only glimpse of daylight.

Sylvie, the "white lady" funeral attendant, walks solemnly past me and places my order of yellow gerberas onto Harriet's coffin.

"Izzy, have you got the photo?"

It's my favourite photo of her. Taken at last year's aged care Easter bonnet parade. Harriet wasn't satisfied till every inch was covered in pom poms and yellow pansies. Her tiny face beaming out from under the bonnet, that's how I will try to remember her. It was such a happy day.

Bossy chubby Harriet became a frail sparrow over the past three months. Just the occasional outburst, a two-year-old temper tantrum, usually over the colour of her cup of tea.

Green suede gloves hide my bleeding sore hands. This week has taken its toll on my fingernails, most are chewed below the quick.

Ooops nearly dropped you.

There you go, Harriet, amidst the gerberas, perfect.

Reassuringly, Silvie rubs my arm, guiding me back to my seat in the middle of the front row. Preferring to be at the back and make a quick getaway, my choice of seating was vetoed by Betty, the head deaconess. Dictating that I sit on the seat opposite the pastor's pulpit, directly in front of Harriet's coffin. Betty has wasted no time stepping into Harriet's shoes as director of church traffic.

Maria and Joe Bartolo, our jolly round Italian neighbours, or eye-taliens, as Harriet calls them, are seated behind me. They are the only people I want to see today.

Emigrating from Sicily in the 1960's, Maria just 20 years old with a new baby daughter and little English, they set up the local pizza parlour, a huge success in a suburb with only one Chinese takeaway. Maria's easy way with the local teenagers and Joe's wood fire oven pizza were a knockout.

Not believing the possibility they could do so well, Harriet was convinced their café was selling drugs, sending money to the Italian mafia.

"Not everybody from Italy is related to the mafia, Harriet dear,"

Dad would mutter under his breath.

Dad was usually a pushover with Harriet, this time he quietly reminded her that they were just hard-working people who deserved their success.

You couldn't have an opinion that differed from Harriet's. Well, you could, but you had to prepare for a battle of words.

Maria and Joe are real people, who eat real food, with a gaggle of kids who are my closest thing to a real family.

Harriet would be mortified if she knew how many times I had gone to Saturday night mass, home with them for a rum toddy to warm us up. Bowls of steaming spaghetti, loaded with garlic and fresh herbs from Maria's garden, which was always twisting its way over our side fence.

After dad died, Maria and Joe were kind to Harriet, but their generosity was not returned. Still, Maria never said an unkind word about my mother. Their generosity of spirit and gentleness was a stand-out in Harriet's hypocritical world.

The Catholics didn't seem to have the restrictions that I did growing up. You can make confession and start another day with a clean slate.

Going to Mass was more like visiting an art gallery. Beautiful paintings, gold ornaments, swinging perfumed handbags and chanting. So mystical to me, after the atmosphere of a Baptist church service. Following Saturday night mass, all the kids were allowed to have an egg cup of strong-smelling wine with just a dash of lemonade.

Alcohol was not on the Baptist agenda. Along with dancing and music (other than hymns). Songs of Praise was Harriet's favourite TV show. Sunday nights at 5pm was my cue to exit, with Harriet humming to favourite hymns and my chores finished, I would run across the shared driveway to Maria's. Six kids would crowd around the black and white telly, watching *Disneyland,* fighting for a seat in their humble but homely sitting room. On strict orders to be back by 6 o' clock for supper before church evening service, leaving behind the mouth-watering scent of Maria's lamb lentil soup was tough.

Harriet was a terrible cook. Our Sunday suppers were usually canned baked beans on toast. Spending all Sunday afternoon typing up the next edition of the Park Orchards

Baptist Bulletin was Harriet's priority.

Sunday lunch followed the morning church service. Bearing more resemblance to a charred blackened gumboot than roast chicken. Supper was just a quick throw-together.

Monthly casserole teas were my favourite church event. Dad and I both loved Mrs Sullivan's porcupine meatballs, tasty little rounds of minced meat stuffed with rice and herbs.

Harriet's attempts at exotic meals swayed between packet Rice a Riso and Vesta curry dinners. I didn't know beans were green till I ate at Maria's.

Saturday was the only day I was allowed to cook. Harriet off on her visits to the sick and elderly, the kitchen became "Izzy's Café." Laden with bowls of fresh herbs from next door, inspired by Maria's Italian cooking, I would try my hardest to concoct us a Saturday night feast.

As soon as Harriet was out of the door, Dad and I would spread out the Saturday Sun Herald. Flipping the pages straight to the middle of the paper, the quiz section, I would start on the code words while dad read the clues for the cryptic crossword.

Taking turns to boil the kettle and top up the teapot, slowly over the years Dad taught me the tricks of the cryptic.

Saturday afternoons were spent chopping and tasting.

Harriet didn't enjoy my culinary efforts, pushing the food around on her plate, grumbling about too many spices.

"Izzy, I could smell the garlic pulling into the driveway, you know what it does to my stomach."

Dad would wink at me. "More for us then, Izzy."

Harriet was herself an immigrant, a ten pound pom who had made the long journey from post war London, just days after she married my father Stan in the late '50s.

Dad already had his round-the-world liner ticket. Harriet should have travelled in the lower class that the ten pound ticket provided. A few hasty letters written from the Mayor of Melbourne, who was a family friend, allowed for Harriet to travel in Dad's 2nd class cabin.

Maybe that trip gave her a sense of unfounded entitlement.

Harriet looked down on our neighbours, after all they didn't speak the Queens English ...

As a teenager Harriet took comfort in her local church, seeking refuge from an alcoholic father and a mother severely affected by post war stress disorder. The London Blitz had claimed many lives in her neighbourhood and nobody could blame her for escaping those memories.

Meeting my father at choir practice was an unanticipated dream.

Just days before her wedding her mother had threatened her, "If you leave and go to that primitive country, you will never hear from us again."

It was no idle threat.

Harriet never heard from her parents, she had to be content with snippets of news held in letters from girlfriends. As the years rolled by the letters dried up.

Stan and Harriet sailed to Melbourne two days after their wedding.

Maria coughs behind me, placing her hand on my shoulder. I turn halfway and give her a small smile. Having her behind me is reassuring. Happy I am wearing the green hat from Machu Picchu that she brought back for me on their last trip.

I think it's disrespectful to wear a hat in church. Along with Harriet's turquoise coffin, we are not sticking with convention today.

The box of coconut Rocher in my bag is comforting, staying warm and eating chocolate is the only way I will get through today. Oh, and a few glasses of Joes' home brew.

Harriet would be turning in her coffin to know that her fridge now contains bottles of chardonnay and gin, no longer hidden away under a pile of clothes in my wardrobe.

Pastor Jean raises her hands. "All stand for the Lord's Prayer."

Jolted back to reality I pop a Raffaello chocolate into my mouth.

Breathe, just breathe.

Silvie and her comrades are standing solemnly, ready to take Harriet on her final journey. Silvie gently takes Harriet's picture off the coffin and hands her to me. Blurred by hot tears rolling down my face I look around behind me, struggling to see Maria. Linking my arm as I reach her we walk together behind the coffin.

Hugging Harriet's photo to my chest it's the hug I waited for that never came.

The "White Ladies" form a line. Wearing their hats, they look like cowgirls. Harriet is lifted skilfully and slid into the hearse full of flowers.

Her coffin looks like a tree with blossom.

"The coffin is beautiful, Izzy, you do your mama proud."

"What will I do now, Maria?" I sob.

"You will find yourself, Izzy, but it takes time."

The hearse is pulling slowly away and I am watching you disappear.

Bye, Mum.

Pastor Jean waits, watching Harriet till the hearse turns out of sight on its journey to the crematorium.

"I hope we will see you at prayer meeting this week, Izzy, you need God's love now, we are all here for you."

"Thank you, Pastor, I will see how I feel. I know that Harriet would appreciate all you have done for her."

Lying seems the best thing right now.

"Perhaps a small donation to the mission fund, Izzy, I know that's what your mother would want."

For fuck's sake ...

What is wrong with these people, my mother has just died!

14

Breathe, breathe.

"Thank you, Pastor, I'll be in touch."

Climbing into Maria's car without a backward glance, I have no intention of ever stepping into this church again.

Izzy's house in suburban Melbourne, Australia

Chapter 2

The call I had been dreading came from the hospital on a Sunday morning at 6.30am. Tossing and turning all night, I knew before I picked up that phone that this was not going to be good news. "Is this Izzy Baker?" Not waiting for an answer, the Matron on my mother's ward spoke the words I was dreading. "I am sorry to tell you that your mother passed away at 4am peacefully."

Even though I could hear the words my mind was numb, I just could not process them.

"You can come in this morning to pick up your mother's things. Would you like to see her again before she's moved to the hospital morgue?"

"Ahh, no thank you, I'll remember her as she was."

I did not want to see Harriet dead.

My sense of guilt was overwhelming. Why hadn't I stayed with her, and not gone home for pizza with Maria?

"It could take days for her to slip away, go and rest," the nurses had assured me.

Harriet died alone.

Joe drove me over to the hospital later that morning. The nurse handed me a plastic bag containing her slippers, dressing gown, orange handbag and the clothes she wore the day the paramedics took her in the ambulance.

It was her lungs that let her down in those final hours. Not responding to antibiotics and suffering massive fluid retention. Harriet pulled the feeding tube out three times.

She wanted to go home, not to our home, but to her heavenly home. When you were Baptist and dying, "Home" was the code word. Pastor Jean leant closer to Harriet to hear those painfully whispered words,

"I want to go Home." Giving Harriet's tiny hand a gentle squeeze the Pastor read from the Bible. Sitting at the end of the bed I was excluded from this private moment.

That little sparrow lying in the bed was a fragile reminder of Harriet, the commander of our ship.

She chose to slip away while I wasn't there, timing it perfectly for the church announcements at that morning's Sunday service.

The last thing she whispered in her barely-there voice,

"Make sure to ring the Pastor first when I go, she will let everybody know."

I really thought she would still be there tomorrow and the next day.

No I love you, or thanks for all your caring, Izzy, you were a wonderful daughter. Nothing, she was gone.

When Pastor Jean made the announcement to the congregation there were gasps of surprise.

"I am very sad to tell you all, Harriet left us in the early hours of the morning, called to the arms of our heavenly father, her years of suffering over."

Most of the congregation knew she was in hospital but this was the eighth visit for Harriet, it had become a monthly occurrence.

Everybody expected her to rise up again, continuing her floral duties and elderly home visits.

Pneumonia was a silent killer and more than her little body could take.

Even in death Harriet was organised.

Pastor Jean already had the funeral plan that Harriet gave her years earlier. Hymns chosen, favourite prayers, short service followed by sandwiches and tea, nothing costly.

There was little for me to do except choose the coffin and grieve for the mother I didn't have in life.

I chose the "The White Ladies" to organise the funeral. The only other funeral parlour in Park Orchards was managed by the McCains. John McCain was rude and his breath always stunk of beer. Harriet would never forgive me if I had put her funeral in their hands.

A week before Harriet's funeral, Silvie the White Lady funeral rep arrived at our house. Stepping through the door and into the lounge room, she whipped out the box of tissues before I had a chance to offer her a cuppa. This was a well-rehearsed scene for her.

Harriet organised Dad's funeral so I had no idea what to expect. Incorrectly assuming there would be some gentle talk to make me feel comfortable, a nice pot of tea. Silvie was perched on the edge of the sofa looking more ready to take flight than administer solace. Glancing frequently at her watch, she was clearly on a tight schedule.

"It's been a busy week, this winter has been a tough one. Will there be a charge from the church for the service, Izzy?" she asked looking up from her watch.

"There had better not be, after the 40 years she just devoted to them," I retorted.

"I guess that's a no then." She ticked another box.

"I will check with the Pastor, I am sure that will be fine. Ok just the coffin to go, I know this is upsetting for you Izzy."

If she thought this was upsetting for me, she didn't show it, pushing the folder across the coffee table leaving a trail in the dust. Housework was never my strong point, with Harriet in hospital for six weeks I had just let it go. Planning to do a spruce around the day before she came home …

I ran my eyes over the coffins on the page.

"Don't you have any others, Silvie?" I asked.

"What do you mean? These are very fine oak coffins with solid brass, silver-plated handles." She looked at me feigning offence.

"I mean, not brown."

"Well, we do have a small coloured range but they are much more expensive."

Sylvie pulled the folder back, thumbing through the pages to the last sheet. This part of the folder was clearly not often used, the pages crisp and clean.

"We have five coloured coffins, but they are 2,000 dollars extra, it's because of the special lacquer, most people go for the oak. I assume your mother is to be cremated?"

"Yes," I whispered.

Not wanting to think about the way the coffins slide behind the curtains. Cremations were creepy. I really didn't know much about death. Does the coffin go into a huge furnace there and then? Or do they save up all the coffins for that day and do a group burning? These questions and more remained unanswered, had Sylvie read my mind she would be shocked.

I had no plans to go to the crematorium, I would say bye to Harriet and the church at the same time.

"Izzy?" Silvie jolted me back to reality.

"We will take the turquoise, please," I said very definitely.

Silvie raised an eyebrow and kept writing.

"I see on our records that your father's ashes are in the rose garden at Park Orchards Crematorium, will I request a space beside them for your mother?"

"Well I suppose so," thinking of poor Dad's peace and quiet. "Sorry, the last week has been such a blur I hadn't even thought about her ashes."

"Leave it all to us, that is what we are here for," she responded.

Sylvie stood up stuffing her coffin folder into her bag as she moved towards the front door.

"It's an unusual choice, but I am sure your mother will appreciate being the only Park Orchards Baptist member to have a green coffin."

"It's turquoise, her favourite colour," I mumbled back at her, thinking of all the rainbow jumpers Harriet had knitted for the African mission children. My last chance to please her. Harriet wouldn't be happy about the cost but she would be setting the trend in coffins.

"Oh, Izzy, one more thing, the payment, assuming the cost will be deducted from Harriet's estate, can you give me your mother's solicitor's details please? We'll forward the death certificate in about three weeks. You'll need that before the Solicitor can commence to disperse Harriet's estate."

The only thing that Harriet and I shared was a love of colour.

She was not spontaneous or prone to spending money on experience. Dad took years to talk her into a cruise to New Zealand.

Imagining that the same young woman sailed 10,000 miles to Australia from England is difficult, aged 30 with her new Aussie husband, twelve weeks of vomiting and a growing concern that maybe her nausea was more than seasickness.

When I was old enough to understand pregnancy, it dawned on me just how soon after their marriage I came into the world. Counting their wedding anniversary to my birthday there were just nine months. Maybe Harriet's resentment towards me started on that long voyage. Whatever, it never went away. I like to think I was conceived in the Suez Canal, it's somehow way more exotic than Park Orchards.

My job of funeral organisation was easy, there were not many people to contact.

Harriet's friends consisted mainly of the church congregation. Val the local hairdresser was a friend of necessity. Harriet would not miss her weekly visit for a wash and perm.

Her only other friends were the Protestant residents at the St Maria Villa for aged care and they were all bedridden.

St Maria's was run by the Catholic church, the only aged care facility in Park Orchards. As head deaconess, Harriet made it her mission to provide date scones and prayers every Saturday morning for the non-Catholic residents. Behind her back Dad and I laughed about them being a captive audience. Most of them deaf to her prayers, but delighted with her scones, though she neglected to mention that they were baked by another member of the ladies committee. Even some of the Catholic residents had started to join her prayer morning, tempted by the waft of buttery date treats.

Five years after we lost Dad, numerous falls, and a case of food poisoning later, the social services lady was still trying to convince Harriet that moving into St Maria's would be her best option. Harriet was having none of it. Determined to get her way as usual she decided that I should move back home as her full-time carer. Then she wouldn't have to pay for the assisted care package. I would do the cleaning cooking and shopping, Harriet reminding me it was my responsibility. Hoping Harriet would tire of this arrangement, I reluctantly agreed.

Receiving the carer's pension was a far cry from my salary as stenographer to Dr Wee, my pet name for the specialist urologist I had worked for since leaving school. I learned quickly at a young age about penile dysfunction and Viagra. Dr Wee's office, located in the Paris end of Collins Street, Melbourne, was prestigious, Harriet loved to tell her friends how well I had done. Glossing over the fact that I worked for a penis doctor and had not even completed my High School Certificate.

After fourteen years in my own humble one bedroom flat in Moonee Ponds, I was again back living under Harriet's rule, in a place that only held bad memories: my bedroom unchanged from its seventies zigzag brown and orange wallpaper. Posters of David Cassidy and Cat Stevens slightly ripped but still taped onto the walls above my bed.

There are no relatives left to mourn her.

My traumatic birth had been enough to be sure that there

would be no more pitter-patter of tiny feet. I gave up hoping for a brother or a sister. Gruesome stories of her thirty hour labour and eventual caesarean delivery were retold enough times to make sure I had no interest in ever going through childbirth.

My father's siblings died years ago, Harriet's only sister Bella lived in France.

I don't know much about my namesake, Aunt Bella. She was twenty years younger than my mother. Must have been a shock for my grandmother, a change of life baby.

Whenever I asked Harriet about her family she seemed sad and reluctant to talk about them. It was as if that part of my mother's life had never happened.

How I wished I had a sister to share secrets with and swap clothes. Couldn't believe Harriet had a sister she never even wrote to. My hopes of ever meeting her were quashed when Harriet announced tearfully that she had just heard her sister had died of ovarian cancer. That was five years ago.

Park Orchards was originally undulating hills covered in apple trees. The oldest home in the area, the villa was originally built by the Italian settlers who had planted the orchards. Now converted to St Maria's Villa for aged care and run by the Catholics. The lush acres eventually sold to form suburban criss-cross streets with houses like boxes, built in the '50s and '60s.

They looked out over the valley to Essendon Airport, now just a bunch of old aircraft hangars rusting away.

One night after work I came home to the sounds of sirens wailing, thick black smoke billowing up over the valley.

A light plane had crashed into one of those little houses, the whole family incinerated while they ate their dinner.

Sounds of a wounded animal came from under my parent's bedroom door.

"Oh my god, what's happening?" Dad not even bothering

23

to rebuke me for taking the Lord's name in vain was a serious sign.

"I've called the doctor, Izzy, your mother is having a breakdown."

Rolling up his sleeves as he came out carrying his bag, Dr Stevens said Harriet would not wake till morning. Severely traumatised by what she had heard, she was now heavily sedated.

"I'll pop back in the morning to see how she is doing."

After he left and with Harriet in a sleepy haze, Dad talked about the bombs and sirens during the blitz on London.

Harriet, just 15 years old, had been a bomb raid warden. Her job and that of many like her was to guide people from their homes down into those dark shelters. Sitting for hours till the overhead sirens ceased.

Those airport sirens sent horrific wartime memories. The screams and stench of burning bodies. Friends that didn't make it.

We call it post traumatic stress disorder now, it has a label. In those days you just had to get on with it. Every man for himself trying to get on with their lives in a war-torn London.

Understanding then how Harriet's need to escape outweighed her fear of losing contact with her parents. Behind that bossy opinionated exterior was a brave young woman.

After two weeks of meals in her bedroom, Harriet rejoined the household. Dad and I were back to our regular positions of soldiers with Harriet as Commander.

1978 plane crashes into local home, Melbourne.

Chapter 3

Isabella is my real name. I love my name. It makes me feel beautiful.

Nicknames stick when you're young. Isabella became Izzy, the boys at school changed it to pissy.

Dad called me bluey, an Aussie nickname for a redhead.

Most people don't even know I am a redhead, thanks to black hair dye. My first weekly salary was spent on hair colouring, the darkest shade I could find, perfect for hiding ginger hair. Freckles and pale skin are harder to hide.

My frizzy locks have been lopped off for as long as I can remember. Probably something to do with frequent bouts of head lice during primary school. Trying to entice my hair past shoulder length just produced dreadlocks that were impossible to untangle. Val, the hairdresser told Harriet she should have my hair cut as short as possible, assuring her it would be the only way to control the tangles and dandruff.

So I looked like a red haired poodle. More like a boy than a girl, an easy target for the bully kids at school. Unfortunately for me, our school uniform was navy blue, which just made the clumps of dandruff stand out even more.

Just when I thought the name calling could get no worse, the boys decided it would be hilarious to call me period head. There was no end to their cruelty.

Taking solace in food, I became a seriously depressed fat dumpling with red frizzy hair.

Our secondary college was a mile walk from home, uphill and across the railway track. It added ten minutes to the journey to walk to the concrete underpass. It wasn't the extra time that made me scrabble up and over those tracks each day. Each school morning I would hold my breath ... Would they be there or not ... I couldn't see them till I turned the corner and then it was too late to go back ... They would stand across the pathway that led out of the tunnel. Forcing me to push my way past their disgusting groping hands.

"Show us your tits, pissy Izzy," trying to grab me, throwing stones as I ran up past the station entrance and out onto the street.

Sometimes they followed me the rest of the way to school yelling out, "Hey Izzy, got your period on?" Getting to school was no relief, most of them were in my maths class. Hearing their sniggering behind me. I sat in the front row so nobody could see my burning cheeks.

I like to think that some of the girls felt sorry for me. None of them would take the chance of walking with me in case they were picked on as well. I didn't blame them for that.

Whoever decided it was a good idea for a group of girls to choose their own netball teams wasn't very good at child psychology. Every sports day, I was the last person to be chosen for a team. Nobody wanted a fat short arse on their side. Whichever team I was on would walk off together, leaving me standing alone.

Telling Dad and Harriet was a waste of time.

Parents didn't go marching up to your school demanding justice in those days. Dad would look sadly at me, and Harriet's response of,

"Izzy, names will never hurt you," stung more than the stones that were thrown at me. Nobody was on my side. Lunch breaks were spent hiding away in the library.

The girls in my class had boyfriends or bitchy girlfriends. Long shiny hair, athletic bodies and hitched their dresses hitched over their belts to show their long legs to the boys.

A week after I started the short cut over the railway track, I came home from school to find a police car in our driveway. Somebody had reported me climbing the fence and crossing the train tracks. Handing Dad the twenty dollar fine, Sergeant O' Brian gave me a stern warning, if I was caught again it would go to court.

After nearly a month of locking myself in my bedroom,

refusing to speak, Dad decided to overrule Harriet.

Fifteen years old, I was just old enough to leave school. Harriet finally agreed, if Dad could help me find a secretarial job, I could leave school. It was jobs for the boys. Dad's Baptist cronies saved me from Park Orchards underpass.

The underpass

Chapter 4

I was a Sunday school rebel.

Our young female teacher told Harriet I was a distraction to the rest of the class. I didn't mean to be disruptive, asking questions was not expected from the younger congregation. It was boring and unbelievable, followed by church service, prayer meetings and Sunday night service. Sundays were the worst day of my week.

It was a huge disappointment to Harriet, I was not baptised. Baptist parents have their babies blessed and pledge an oath to the church to raise them as good Christians. As young teenagers they are urged to take Jesus into their hearts and themselves pledge a life to the church. Harriet never gave up hope that one day I would see the light and feel the calling and be baptised. Nothing could have been further from my mind.

Our pastor announced that Billy Graham, the famous evangelist preacher, was making a world tour with Melbourne on his agenda. Harriet was so excited …

"I really don't want to come Harriet," I protested, as much as a ten-year old can.

"Well I've paid $40 for the tickets, and that's that. They're doing a mass baptism at the end."

Poor Harriet, hoping the atmosphere of thousands of God-botherers would urge me to become baptised.

The three of us made the trip to the MCG, along with hundreds of others, crowding on to trains at Flinders Street Station. Harriet brought our lunch from home.

The scent of hot salty chips from station vendors was making my stomach growl.

"It's daylight robbery for food at the MCG, NO, we will take our flask and sandwiches." Dried out ham and cheese sandwiches with weak warm coffee was our lot.

Dad whispered we would sneak out and get a hot dog, he

knew this was not an easy day for me.

It was 40 degrees that day, St John's ambulance treated hundreds for heat exhaustion.

Fainting with sunstroke I needed to be brought home before the service ended. Secretly I think Dad was glad he had an excuse to get home and watch the cricket. A rare occasion when being a sun-sensitive redhead worked in my favour.

That was Harriet's last real attempt at converting me. My days of Sunday school finally over, but still expected to attend two church services ...

I wondered about the afterlife. In fact, I was fascinated by it.

Where did we go after death? Surely not up in the clouds with all the billions of others that had died. What happened to our spirits? The spirit world, mysticism, tarot, numerology, runes, guardian angels, astrology, star signs, past lives, symbology, white witches.

Our library only had three books on Esoterics and I had read them all, dating back to 14th century Europe. Tarot cards captured my imagination.

Having croissants in Lulu's, my favourite French café, was a brekky treat before work. It was like stepping into a Parisian world. The rich aroma of just-ground coffee, baked baguettes hot from the oven. Black and white photos of a misty Seine, warm and cosy sitting under the stunning chandelier.

This morning, flipping open the local paper while I sipped my creamy coffee, my eyes caught the words, "Esoterics."

"Diploma of Esoteric Studies."

"Melbourne TAFE College will be commencing its Diploma of Esoteric Studies with the first intake to commence March 1984.

Lectures to be held in the Bourke Street auditorium.

Mondays Wednesdays and Fridays at 6.30pm

Three year diploma course."

"Mrs Elly Richardson, head of the Australian Tarot Guild, will lead the course, together with guest lecturers.

Numbers limited enrolments to close Jan 30, 1984."

As luck would have it I worked just around the corner in Collins Street, plenty of time for a quick supper at Gino's Italian Café before the lectures started. The last train from Spencer Street Station to Park Orchards left at 9.05pm, so running down Bourke St or jumping on a tram I could just make it.

That chance sighting in the Melbourne Gazette put me onto my Karmic path.

Fifteen years ago I stepped up onto the podium to receive my "Diploma of Esoteric Studies" from the Dean of the university.

Looking out into the rows of faces, I knew there was nobody there to cheer for me, but nothing could diminish how proud I felt that evening.

Dad and Harriet knew about my course, but in interest of harmony we rarely spoke about it. Occasionally Dad would ask me how it was going, Harriet would jump in with her devil's work speech.

The world of tarot became my unspoken passion. Three nights a week of transportation to another place.

Coming home on graduation night, my aura was glowing. That wink from Dad meant the world to me.

There started my dream to one day run an Esoteric bookshop.

A beautiful welcoming space where I could give my clients readings over a glass of wine or coffee. Full to the brim with cards, runes and crystals. Books overflowing with magical stories from medieval Europe. Celtic music and angel cards. Somewhere to leave the world behind and listen to your inner voice.

The years have come and gone, but my cards still carry unwaning curiosity and mysticism. They are my constant companions never letting me down. Wrapped in a silky scarf, adorned with Celtic images from the Book of Kells, brought back by a work friend from a trip to Dublin. Nestled in the bottom of my tapestry bag, my little dream woven around them waiting for the opportunity to surface.

Tarot is a window to your soul, a reflection of your thoughts, sometimes a message from the spirit world.

There is no box to tick for Buddhism on most forms, but it's the closest I can come to finding what I believe. It's not all shaved heads and chanting. Harriet confusing the Hare Krishnas in Bourke Street for Buddhists.

Buddhists believe that lessons in life are learned over many lives. Living in the moment, trying to have no expectations. Kindness to all living beings.

The hypocrisy of so many religions, forcing their beliefs onto others, killing in the name of God. Surely kindness is more important in our world than what country you are born in?

If God was truly everywhere, why did we need to spend hours sitting in a Baptist Hall to make contact with him?

Points all lost on Harriet.

Three months ago, waiting till I could hear Harriet snoring softly, tucked up for her afternoon nap. Knowing I had two hours before she would ring her bell for tea, I lifted my silky bundle, closed the front door softly, heading across our driveway to Maria.

It was early April, we were having an Indian summer, Maria's door was open to let in the afternoon breeze.

Tapping gently, I called out, "It's just me Maria."

"Come in Bella," (her nickname for me made me feel special.)

Maria was in the kitchen stirring a large bubbling pot.

"Here, taste this." She lifted the wooden spoon to my lips.

"Ouch, that's hot but yummo, it's delicious." Licking the passata from my mouth.

34

"Stay for dinner if you like."

"I can't, Maria, you are so sweet to ask, I worry too much about leaving Harriet. Last time I wasn't there she fell out of bed, I am sure she just does it to give me a guilt trip."

"It's hard for you, Izzy, you're a good girl to your muma."

"Time for cards, Maria?" I winked at her.

"Always," she beamed back at me.

"Let's sit outside in the warm," she led the way through the broken fly screen door and onto the back verandah.

"Oh Maria, you are such a good friend to me, what would I do without you?" I smiled at her.

Maria cleared away Joe's ashtray from the porch table, tut tutting, "Filthy habit."

"Wait, we give a little wipe, you not put your pretty scarf in the dusty."

Maria's Sicilian accent so charming, her English words rolling off her tongue, in her unique style.

"What about a little glass of bubbles?" not waiting for an answer, heading towards Joe's outdoor fridge.

"Ok, just one, don't want Harriet to smell it." I laugh.

Usually, my readings were for Maria, always worried about one of her six children or four grandchildren.

Today I really wanted the reading to be for me.

Maria and I both knew time was running out for Harriet, the past months had seen her get weaker and weaker. Five years since moving back home and having a proper job, I am despairing, who on earth will employ me again?

My confidence has been sapped, all I feel good for is cooking, cleaning and chauffeuring Harriet to and fro between church and hospital specialist appointments.

As I am unable to drive, she insists I go in the taxis with her, she worries that the mostly immigrant drivers won't understand her. They are always so sweet and kind to her, even though she usually bumps the side of their cars with her walking frame. Going shopping with her is a nightmare, she is like a bull in a china shop.

It's very hard to be subjective about your own tarot reading. I am glad of Maria's insight. Her funny ideas about the symbology of the cards, often leave us in stitches of laughter. No matter what, she is always completely honest.

Maria plumps her big bottom on the rickety garden chair opposite me, we both take a sip from our glasses, I love the sweet bubbles swirling around in my mouth. For a moment I can forget about my responsibilities lying at home.

Feeling relaxed I untie my precious bundle, spreading out the Celtic scarf. Shuffling the cards I close my eyes, thinking about Harriet.

"What will happen, angels, when she goes?"

Splitting the cards into two decks I choose the biggest pile.

"Just like you, Izzy, glass half full." Maria gives me a wink.

She's right, I am a dreamer and usually positive around her.

Crumbling inside and too scared to admit to her what a mess I've become.

I spread the biggest deck of cards out face down, choosing three cards I think to myself, so what do you have for me angels?

Slowly I turn the cards over one by one.

Ten of Swords – Defeat, end of painful situation, crisis.

This card looks so bleak the body in the picture lays with ten daggers thrust into it.

Maria looks at me sadly but doesn't say a word.

Wheel of Fortune – New chapter, make a change, good luck, karma, turning point. The rota can take you up on a new journey or down again if you're not careful.

This is a card of promise, it means the start of a new cycle. Could I dare to do things differently than the past?

Two of cups – Unified love, partnership, attraction.

Ahhhh, Maria lets out a pleasing response.

I looove this card.

Maria was a romantic, her favourite movie *Cinderella*.

"You wait see, my Izzy, it will be your turn soon."

Despite Maria's optimism, it's hard for me to imagine myself ever having a relationship with anybody other than my cards.

Tarot reading.

Ten of Swords, The Wheel of Fortune, Two of Cups .

Rider-Waite deck

Chapter 5

Three weeks after my reading with Maria, I arrived home weighed down with groceries. The bus stop was just across from our house. I turned the corner to see Maria running to meet me.

Parked in our driveway was an ambulance, our front door was open.

"Harriet has fallen in the bathroom they think she has a broken hip," Maria says, out of breath.

"What the heck, I have only been gone for an hour," I reply.

"She pushed her emergency buzzer, when there was no answer to the phone, they sent the paramedics." Maria puts her hand on my arm as if she knows this is the start of the end.

Running into the hallway I can see Harriet tightly secured on the trolley.

"It looks like a break, love, she has oedema, bad fluid retention." The Ambo's know me well, this is one of many call-outs for Harriet.

"I will be right behind you Harriet," I whisper to her, but she's already dozy from the pethidine injection to relieve the pain.

Climbing into the back of the ambulance, all I can do is hold her tiny bony hand.

Six weeks later, in hospital after an operation to pin Harriet's hip, she contracted pneumonia. Sounding like squeaky Minnie Mouse and not eating, her blocked airway was preventing proper swallowing, causing food to move into her lung. One day she was whispering to me and the next she was in a coma.

A week later she was gone.

Thinking back on my reading with Maria, this was the ten of swords. The end of a crisis and five years of a life that I hadn't chosen. Wondering if things would have been different if I had a brother or sister to help with the load of caring for Harriet. Would I have stood up for myself? Sorry I have an important job, I can't possibly move back home.

Who am I kidding, not myself, I would have done the same and felt responsible. Oh, to not have such a guilt complex.

Apart from my esoteric studies, there has been no chance to be who I would like to be. Lost with no purpose.

Three weeks after the funeral, Annie the kindly social worker popped in to see me. She says it's normal to feel like you are drifting, cut loose in time. Losing a loved one is like losing a part of yourself.

How can I tell her I didn't love Harriet? My life made so difficult by her selfishness. I respected her for the changes that she made in her life, that can't have been easy, but incapable of showing love or affection she built a wall around herself. Shutting me out.

If I am relieved she has gone, why do I feel so sad?

Without Harriet's 6am alarm, for her first cup of tea, I am sleeping till all hours of the morning. Luxuriating in heating without the timer, drinking way too much wine, playing loud music, trying to think what to do with my life. Thank the angels for Maria, who is worried I am not eating properly, sending Joe over with bowls of minestrone and invites for supper.

Indulging in Chardonnay and chocolates is not helping my spreading belly. I haven't dressed for days, it's easier to hide under my shabby dressing gown.

"It's OK to wallow for a while, but don't let yourself drown, Izzy. There is a whole big world out there just waiting for you. Remember your Wheel of Fortune?" Maria draws a circle in the air and gives me a little smile.

Dreams of travel to exotic places are still tucked away in a tiny pocket in my heart. Always a reason why they couldn't take flight. Moving from home at 17 takes every little cent. It took years for me to work my way up to a halfway decent salary. All my wages going on rent and food. Still, I wouldn't have it any other way, no way was I going back to live under Harriet's command. I would rather be broke, living with my dreams than suffer her hypocrisy.

I want to be brave like the heroines in history I love to read about.

Joan of Arc, just nineteen when she marched into the pages of French history leading her army to glory against the English.

Eleanor of Aquitaine, Queen of France and England.

All so inspiring compared to the dull history of the Australian penal colonies.

Even Harriet, leading her neighbours to safety aged just 15 in the blitz. Aged 25, Dad had ventured round the world.

What the fuck is wrong with me ... I am nearly forty and I have been nowhere ...

Maria pours the boiling water over my ginger lemon teabag. Wishing it was a gin and tonic, I have my head in my hands.

"Izzy, Izzy." Maria puts her arm around my shoulders. "Perhaps you could think about our offer to buy your house?"

My house ... Those words still don't seem real. A life dictated by circumstance till now, I have to stop making excuses and face my fear.

Always the guilt-ridden dutiful daughter scared to upset Harriet's apple cart, scared to be truthful to myself about what I want to do, hating myself for being so spineless.

Maria's daughter Gina wants to be close to her mother, it makes perfect sense for her to be next door. Joe and Maria could expand their veggie garden planting the olive and fig trees they had been talking about for years.

It would certainly boost my bank balance, maybe I could plan a trip to all the medieval cities I dream and read about.

Travelling on my own would be scary and exciting all

rolled into one.

Could I be brave enough? Just thinking these thoughts sends shivers of excitement and fear through my veins.

I need a plan.

OK baby steps.

Tomorrow is going to be the start of my Wheel of Fortune, a new chapter.

"You' re right Maria, starting with a healthy breakfast and no sleeping in." I give her a little smile.

Maria adds, "Making an appointment to meet with the local real estate agent for a house valuation?"

"OK," I agree.

Supper with Joe and Maria. That's enough for one day.

Promising myself, no wine or Raffaellos till Harriet's room is cleared tomorrow. I fall asleep to the thoughts of medieval chateaux and French cafes.

My Dad high on a snow-capped mountain comes to my dreams, smiling, young, healthy and strong. As I climb towards him he stretches out his hand to me: "Come on, Bluey, you can do anything."

Joan of Arc, 1412 – 1431

Chapter 6

Thanks to the Queen and my mother I am now the proud recipient of a UK passport.

It arrived yesterday by special delivery.

Burgundy and gold lettering on the cover open up to the most awful passport photo in the whole wide world. Usually wearing a hat to cover my frizzy curls, I knew this was not going to be a good photo.

"Hat off, no smiling, hair behind your ears." Joan our post office assistant was enjoying every bit of my discomfort.

Harriet's solicitor has at least been good for something. Her knowledge of the act of succession means I have been able to apply for UK Citizenship. Thank God for the European Union.

Europe has just opened its gates to me.

Isabella Baker you are a citizen of the world.

Maria and Joe have signed the contract to buy Harriet's house. Delighted, they are already making plans for the garden. Just so happy that Gina and her cherub children will be living next door.

The agent's valuation of $400,000 seems unbelievable for a little box in the northern suburbs of Melbourne.

Dad's advice of buying bricks and mortar is ringing true.

He would not believe that his humble purchase of 5,000 pounds in the 60's has turned into such a considerable sum.

Lack of housing, and a growing number of young families who can't afford to make a start in posh southern suburbs, mean that northern suburbs like Park Orchards are in demand.

Joe and Maria are like my family, I can't ask that much money. So, we settle on $350,000.

My family have little longevity, this seems like such a lot of money, enough to see out my days.

There is a comfort from not having expectations. Just blow

with the wind, well now I can.

Anne, my favourite esoterics lecturer, always said, "If you just make one decision, then it will make room for the rest to follow. Unclutter your mind, open the doors to change and good luck."

First things first, tackling this house …

Maria and Joe are not in a hurry for the house, but I need to give myself a deadline, otherwise I will spend months and still not have a plan.

October sounds good. Eeeeeek.

A few months away, time to lose weight, buy new clothes, sort out my head, get the guts to do something with my life. Where to go?

Maria's suggestion of throwing a dart at a map is not that appealing. I might end up in Siberia.

Italy would be amazing only five hours on the train from France, growing up with Maria's Sicilian stories it's tempting.

Working all those years in Collins Street surrounded by haute couture and French antiques I have dreamed what it must be like to live in France.

Watching continental rail journeys, the romance of a steam train coming into a European station.

Time wasting is something I am very good at, daydreaming is not moving any of these boxes.

Harriet was an organised hoarder.

Boxes and boxes of electricity and gas accounts are waiting in the shed. Scared to throw things in the rubbish in case somebody stole her identity.

Days have been spent filling the skip. That's the easy part.

Putting off my parents' bedroom is not an option anymore, with just a week till Maria and Joe get the key. Gina will move in next month and they really want to start peeling off the '70s wallpaper and give it a freshen up.

Not wanting to rush me they have insisted I can stay in

their spare room for as long as I need.

My father's closest possessions still sit neatly on his side of the bed. Reading glasses sitting in the tiny drawer. His books replaced by a copy of the New Testament compliments of Harriet.

This is taking hours longer than I thought it would. Each little folder giving up precious memories. Gently I place all his things into a box and put it to one side, unable to throw them away. Maria said she will keep them for me.

All I take is the black-and-white photo of us together on the sand at Torquay. Smiling under his heavy black framed glasses, me in frills and sun-cream.

Dad dropped dead aged 59, a blood clot had travelled to his brain. "Nobody could have predicted it," the surgeon said.

He was brain dead, unresponsive, but still breathing. Harriet sure of a miracle would not let the hospital take him from the breathing apparatus. I sat with him for a week, holding his hand, talking to him. Knowing his spirit was already soaring on his next journey. Heartbroken that our dream to share an adventure together had been taken from me.

Sometimes I catch a smell of his aftershave and I know he is around me. Then he is gone again.

Oh Dad, it was supposed to be you and me.

Just a little girl, he filled my head with stories of his travels. I loved touching the little silver Colosseum that sat on our fireplace mantle, beside two little black elephants all the way from India. A young man with dreams of adventure, before he had met Harriet in London, how his life changed. From world traveller young and carefree, to family responsibilities and a difficult wife.

Dad worked hard to give Harriet the life she wanted. New house in the suburbs, a car, plenty of clothes to fit her forever changing body size.

Accounts assistants' salaries didn't stretch to Harriet's

excesses, so three days a week Dad did the coal run. No wonder he used to fall asleep over his dinner. Up at 3am on the back of a truck shovelling coal into sacks, home again to soak in the bath, porridge and a rush to catch the 7am train into the city.

We both thought Harriet would go first. High blood pressure, size 24 from years of loving soft drinks and Tim Tams her favourite chocolate biscuits. The doctor said she was putting her heart under pressure. Constantly lecturing her about the damage that diabetes would do to her organs.

Oh God, I am turning into her. Overweight, chewed nails, frizzy hair. Waaaah. I hate myself.

Remembering a promise to myself that I would not have a wine till this room is finished, I settle on just one Raffaello, there are two left in the silver tray in the kitchen. Oh what the heck, one or two. I could start my new eating regime tomorrow.

Humming to the sounds of Ella Fitzgerald, I press on to finish clearing Harriet's wardrobe. Squashed full of cheap vinyl handbags, each discarded containing old train tickets and out-of-date health cards, shopping lists and old church bulletins. Nothing interesting.

Zipping open the last bag and hoping for a $50 note, I see an envelope slotted into a side pocket. Different to the usual business letters it catches my curiosity.

The pink envelope is postmarked Montmorillon France, October 1994. Two sheets of folded rice paper flutter like a butterfly to the floor. Scooping them up carefully, unfolding them gently.

32 Rue Puits Cornet
Montmorillon 86500
Poitou Charente
France
October 12 1994

My dear Harriet

If you're reading this letter it is because I have passed to the spirit world. My diagnosis of ovarian cancer has been a shock, but allowed me to spend precious moments in my favourite pursuits. Soon I will be too weak to leave my bed. The doctor has said it will be quick, he will assist me with pain. I can't bear to spend my final days without colour in a sterile hospital room, Sophie my darling friend of these past fifteen years is a trouper, trying her sweetest to stay cheery. I have asked, that she not send this letter till I am gone. The last letter you sent to me in London is still treasured. Although I wrote to you many times you never replied.

Hearing little of your life since you sailed away from us all those years ago, I can only hope that your new life in Australia brought you the happiness that I have found here in Montmorillon.

A chance finding of a special place and special people, I feel blessed. Sophie will attend to all the messiness of my death. You need not feel any duty or worry.

Our childhood games still flit in and out of my memories.

Our journeys so very different.

I hope this letter finds you, Harriet.

Till we meet again,

Your loving sister Bella

Indian memories

Chapter 7

Dreaming of nasty boys chasing me through school corridors, I am relieved to wake to Cat Stevens soft brown eyes looking down on me.

Buzzzzzz Buzzzzzz buzzzzzzz. Rolling over I look at my clock, shit it's 10am, the doorbell rings out impatiently.

Leaping out of bed, snatching my bathrobe off the floor, tying it quickly around me. Covered in red wine stains it's not for public appearance. Pushing past stacked boxes blocking the doorway, fumbling with the latch on the chain I peek through the tiny space.

"Ah yes, can I help you?"

"Well if you're Isabella Baker you can." The postman is waving a registered letter in his hand.

"Sorry, love, you will have to sign for this."

Opening the wire door enough for him to shove through the signature pad. Grasping the pen I squiggle my name.

"Have a good day, sorry to wake you," he smiles as he heads down the driveway.

My bed hair and smudged mascara a dead give-away. Experimenting with my new French look, makeup and I are strangers.

Flicking on the kettle and turning over the envelope I see the familiar stamp of the solicitors' office in Moonee Ponds.

Harriet's death certificate.

Memories of those last few days come flooding back to me.

Welling up with tears I pour the boiling water onto my coffee.

Harriet was not a nurturing mother but she was somebody. Now I have nobody.

What am I thinking?

Running away to France. My French is rubbish. Three months of French lessons hardly make me fluent.

Most books I read say that if you just try to speak a few

words of French, people are very friendly and mostly speak English. Well, they learn it in school so surely their English is better than my French.

Wishing I had not swapped French class for a secretarial elective all those years ago.

According to the man on continental rail journeys we already know 5,000 French words, English comes from French.

All I have to do is practice my accent … naturally is *naturellement,* comfortable is *comfortable,* certainly is *certainement.*

"Oui, oui, oui, Monsieur, je suis très comfortable."

Laughing out loud at my own silliness brightens my mood for a moment.

Dad breaks in on my thoughts. "Stop it, stop it, Izzy, you can be brave."

Harriet was brave all those years ago ...

Is Bella's letter calling me to France? Is this my Wheel of Fortune? Chasing a dead aunt's dream is madness, what if there is something there for me? Just to know something about my family. Knowing I am so different to Harriet, perhaps I take after Bella? If I could just find her friend Sophie, she might help me to fill in the gaps.

Having a catalyst makes my decision easier. It's a place to start my dream. The alternative of living the rest of my life in Park Orchards, fills me with dread. Drifting around Europe where nobody knows me, I can be whoever I want.

Bella, as a twenty-five-year old, travelled to France, why had she decided to settle in Montmorillon?

Dragging my notepad through the clutter on the kitchen table I flick through to my last library notes.

Montmorillon, population 7,200
Built by the Romans in 890 AD.
Medieval Cité de L'Ecrit, town of writers.

Situated on the Gartempe River in the Poitou Charente region of Central France. The real France, known for its lush farming regions and friendly locals.

Sitting in the shadow of the Notre Dame Eglise, well known by historians for its frescoes depicting the life of St Catherine of Alexandria, now UNESCO listed, awaiting restoration.

Laurent Chapelle burial place of Lord Montmorillon.

I knew I recognised that name, Lord Montmorillon was the Captain of Joan of Arc's army. To think my aunt had lived in a place that held such importance in the pages of French history.

Looking again at the printed page from the travel agent.

Could I make this really happen?

Melbourne Tullamarine Airport to Paris Charles De Gaulle Airport.

Montparnasse Paris to Poitiers – SNCF fast train 2.5 hours or CDG Airport rail station to Poitiers. 1.75 hours.

Change at Poitiers station for local train.

Poitiers – Montmorillon 40 minutes.

Looking at the words on the page it sounds so easy.

Well at least Montmorillon has a railway station. Harriet always picked on me for not getting my driving licence. Honestly, I was scared witless about driving after being a passenger in the car with my mother. After three attempts at going for her licence, her driving instructor suggested perhaps an automatic licence would suit her better. Fourth time lucky she became the proud owner of a Victorian driving licence.

It was a miracle that Dad and I were not victims of Harriet's driving.

Her slow cognitive skills combined with poor distance judgement meant we had many near misses. Walking and train travel were our preferred modes of travel. I would rather get the bus back from the station after work than let Harriet collect me.

Contracting Epilepsy after a measles outbreak in the 1930's, Dad had never been allowed to drive.

In those early days in Park Orchards, the local buses were so unreliable, Harriet wanted a car. It was a status symbol in our neighbourhood.

Me not being a driver rules out hire cars, I hate buses. Since watching *Speed*, where Keanu Reeves saves the day, I can't take a bus without imagining it careering out of control, jumping into the oncoming traffic. Not to mention getting stuck beside the most boring person in the whole wide world. At least on a train you can walk around and have a glass of wine.

Visualising myself, glass of Cote Du Rhone in my hand, French countryside rolling past.

All I have is a name, Sophie le Foy, an address, 32 Rue Puits Cornet. It was five years ago since Harriet received the letter. Madame Le Foy might have moved, I have to try. It gives me purpose, my family is gone, but I so want to know more about Bella, the aunt I never knew.

Thinking how rude it would to just turn up, I scratch out a quick note. I don't want Sophie (if I can even find her) to think I expect anything of her. Maybe I can take her out to lunch and we can talk about Aunt Bella. Staying a week or so, seeing where the mood takes me.

20 Summer Ave
Park Orchards
Victoria
Australia
Dear Madame Le Foy,
    You don't know me, I am your friend Bella's niece. Bella never met me as I was born in Australia. I know that years after my

mother left the family home in London, Aunt Bella travelled to France. My mother Harriet and Bella were not close, but as I have no siblings I would love to know more about my mother's family.

Harriet my mother has recently passed away, so I have decided to take at least a year and explore Europe. Hopefully starting in France.

I will find accommodation on arrival and certainly don't want to intrude on your time. Maybe just a lunch and chat over a glass of wine. I hope to hear from you warm regards,

Isabella Baker (Izzy)

It's a start. If I can't locate her I will just get back on the train heading down to Bordeaux, a big city where I can lose myself.

Beautiful wine, cheese, wonderful food. Happy I have a plan, I snap shut my notepad, humming walking into the bathroom.

The face staring back at me from the mirror looks less stressed than a month ago. Baby steps are progress.

Tomorrow I will take the plunge and book the flight. Eeeeeek.

Chapelle St Laurent, Montmorillon

Chapter 8

My chance finding of Bella's letter and Maria's encouragement have spurred me on to make some decisions.

"If you get there and you don't like it, just book a ticket and come home," Maria makes it sound breezy easy.

"On the other hand, if you decide to stay a few months somewhere, Joe and I could come to visit…"

It's been ages since Joe and Maria have had a holiday. I think she wants to use this as a good opportunity for a little break.

Having faith in my Wheel of Fortune, I hand over the largest cheque I have ever written to Mandy, my booking agent at Moonee Ponds Travel Centre. Swallowing down my excitement I couldn't wait to get back to Maria, for a tiny glass of Chardy to celebrate probably the most amazing step I had ever taken.

This would be the last cheque I would write, now being the proud owner of an ATM debit card. The bank says it will be much easier to use than travellers' cheques. Most of Europe changed over last year to euros. It must have been so much harder when my Dad travelled, with so many different currencies. I feel like it's cheating in a way.

The last few weeks have sped past. My Wheel of Fortune is in motion. Between doing heaps of research about great places to visit in France, my new health regime, and French lessons, there seems little time for much other than eight hours sleep.

Park Orchards' smallish hills make the perfect training ground, I am trying really hard to walk at least two hours a day.

Nearly all the old medieval French cities and towns were fortified. Huge stone walls constructed up high to guard the surrounding areas. Splendid chateau's guarding their people. Cobblestone streets winding past shuttered reminders of a time long ago. Constantly picturing the hilly villages, it's been so much easier to get motivated to lose some weight.

Tomorrow I will spend my last day in Park Orchards staying with Joe and Maria. Not trusting myself to have an early night and stay sober.

It's such an early start with an 8am flight, my ticket issues warnings about late check- ins, and I need to be at Tullamarine airport by 5am. Sweet Joe is driving me to the airport. Leaving early, still in darkness while the streets still sleep makes it all the more exciting.

Maria doesn't like goodbyes, only hellos, so I will hug her tight before we leave. My good luck charm, she has loved me like a child of her own.

Mandy, my new best friend at the travel agency has filled my head with so much helpful information.

European trains nearly all have five or six steps up into the carriage. All 5 foot nothing of me, make anything over 10 kilos a struggle. So, even though I am allowed 20 kilos of luggage I have decided to keep it simple. It will be autumn and chilly when I arrive in Paris.

Travelling in jeans, jumper, coat and runners leaves my tiny case free for my diary, undies, socks, toiletries and three changes of clothes. Mandy assures me, walking off the plane, everything with me, free as a bird, no waiting around packed carousels will ease the stress at the other end. Straight through customs and hello my adventure.

My red tapestry handbag is roomy, easily holding my tarot cards, passport, wallet, novel, toothbrush, not forgetting my new purchase of a travel alarm clock. The *"Lady of the Rivers,"* will be perfect reading for my long flight. If I find myself seated beside a chatterbox, I will bury my head into my book.

All I have to do is check in and ask the angels for an aisle seat.

No climbing over people to get out of my seat, the way my butterflies are feeling, I am expecting to be a frequent visitor to the tiny aeroplane loo.

Not hearing back from Madame Le Foy has been a disappointment, but it's only one tiny glitch, it's just a small part of my trip. I have to stay optimistic, I will be able to find her. How hard could it be? Somebody must have heard of her, even if she no longer lives at the same address.

Imagining a pretty French girl who delivers the post to all the Montmorillonaise on an old-fashioned bicycle, knowing everybody by first name.

"It will be alright in the end and if it's not alright it's not the end," I have to keep telling myself.

With the image of the Eight of Wands, Tarot travel card, foremost in my mind, I snuggle down under Maria's handmade patchwork blanket which feels so comforting. Nervous butterflies still buzzing around my stomach. Hoping they are a good omen, I think of my beautiful Dad. Sending him a silent kiss and hoping he is around me on this journey. Stay with me Dad, I love you.

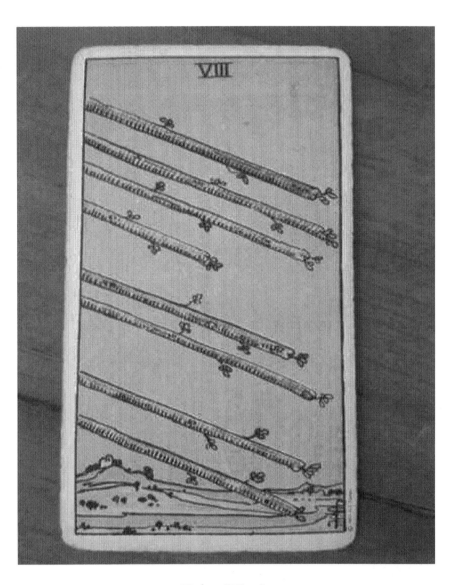

Eight of Wands

Rider-Waite Tarot deck

Chapter 9

They say, as hyperthermia takes hold of your body, you actually start to feel warm. Your mind takes control shutting down your pain receptors, spreading a warm glow through your veins.

Why can't that happen for fear?

At that moment of absolute nauseating panic, why can't our brain make us suddenly feel like Joan of Arc, able to march on in and take on the world.

My first three days in Paris have been delightful and relatively easy.

Pierre, the manager of "La Petite Chambre Hotel," has been so helpful, pretending to understand my bad French. Just ten minutes' walk away from the station I will depart from for Poitiers. Tucked away in Rue Daguerre, a cosmopolitan walkway lined with flower sellers, fruit stalls, tiny bistros and bars.

Pierre helped me with directions to the Catacombs of Paris, laying beneath Montparnasse, spooky tunnels filled with the bones taken from the cemeteries in 18th century Paris.

Not wanting to undo my weight loss, knowing I couldn't resist all the tasty temptations, I walked the five kilometres over the Seine and up through the right bank to the Sacré Coeur. Up thousands of steps overlooking Paris. Onto Montmartre and Moulin Rouge. Pinching myself finding it hard to believe I am actually in Paris, the *City of Love*.

Three months ago, I couldn't have walked down to the local shop without getting puffed. Stopping frequently, bowls of steaming hot chocolate or coffee are delivered outside cafés to tiny pavements, tables filled with aspiring writers and artists. So easy to imagine Hemingway's 1930s.

My last afternoon I wandered through Montparnasse cimetière, wanting to visit Simone Beauvoir's resting place. My 20th century heroine. Such an interesting; inspiring woman. Since reading her novel *"Memories of a Dutiful Daughter,"* I couldn't help but feel similarities in our lives. Her mother was a rigidly moral Catholic, her father a loving very ethical pagan. Originally promised to the convent she renounced her faith. Caught in endless disputes between her parents, she ended up becoming an intellectual. She was bisexual but lived with one man for fifty years. Never marrying and having endless love affairs, she was even charged with seducing female students she was teaching at university. Loving that she challenged the world to be herself. Now buried wearing her lover's silver ring.

Finding her resting place was easy, in a very grey cemetery her tomb stands out, covered in fresh flowers, red lipstick marks on her gravestone, Metro tickets held down by smooth stones as reminders of her visiting admirers. Standing quietly, thinking of her courage to be herself in a man's world.

Tonight, a final special Parisian dinner at La Petite Assiette, recommended by Pierre. Tomorrow is another first, and I need a good night's sleep before I tackle the French fast trains.

Montparnasse Station is massive. This is like stepping into another world. Garbled announcements in French are bellowing out over loud speakers, mixed with security warnings in English and Italian. Two months of French lessons have not prepared me for this onslaught. Gendarmes with hands on automatic weapons are not like the approachable Aussie coppers.

Escalators everywhere don't seem to lead anywhere. People everywhere rushing all around me. Bursting for a pee and feeling rising panic, I decide to take refuge in McDonalds, at least I can point to the overhead menu and find the toilet.

Even "Maccas" is more civilised in France. Tiny buttery ham and Roquefort croissants line the serving shelf, ready for hungry Parisians rushing getting to work, wafts of coffee and sweet *tarte tatin*. Large windows look out over the pedestrian walk, tempting me to stay for hours and people-watch, it would be easy to sit here and not get on the train.

McDo, as the Parisians call it, does so well in Paris, because they treat it as a dining experience, not a fast food outlet. Feeling safe in this cocoon seated on a comfy sofa, I am tempted to go back to "La Petite Chambre" my Montparnasse *chambre d'hôte*.

This should be so exciting getting on a fast train in Europe. The start of my French country journey. Eeeek. Trying to swallow down rising nausea, I reach into my bag pulling out the paper ticket for the hundredth time just to reassure myself. Double counting the 250 euros remaining, pushing it securely out of the reaching fingers of pickpockets.

Train 5222, Montparnasse to Poitiers departing 10.04, taking a deep breath I walk through the auto McDo doors into Montparnasse madness.

Fighting my way past wheelie suitcases and bulging backpacks. Hundreds of commuters resting weary feet are sitting on top of upturned suitcases staring at the massive overhead screen. Looking up to the heavens nearly all the arrivals listed are waiting for platform numbers. Scrolling down the list of departures, I eventually see it, 5222 Bordeaux St Jean. Well if I fall asleep or miss my Poitiers change, ending up in Bordeaux is not too bad.

Leaving, "La Petite Chambre" my aptly named bargain hotel was difficult this morning, tiny but cosy. My home away from home for three days. Unable to reach the loo without climbing over my suitcase, burning my bottom on the radiator, but only down the road from Montparnasse station one of the busiest train stations in the world.

Waving sadly goodbye to Pierre, the jolly concierge, assuring him I would come to stay again when I returned to Paris.

Broadcasts that unattended bags will be confiscated boom out over the speakers. Buzzing conversations, odours from sweaty bodies mixed with just baked croissants. Everybody is in a hurry, welcome to Paris.

Worried I will miss my platform call I keep glancing through the rows of departures. Zurich, Rome, La Rochelle, Lille, Milan, Toulouse. Its mind-blowing, hundreds of destinations. Flashing between arrivals and departures. Suddenly there is a mass exodus, green 24 lights up beside Bordeaux St Jean. Eeeeek, that's me. Standing on my scarf I trip on the wheels of my case, shite, just ten minutes to get to platform 24.

Turning onto the platform I am a bee in a swarm of people, buzzing its way along, slowing thinning out as bodies clamber aboard carriages, passing and pushing heavy valises. Well-meaning relatives clogging up the spaces to wave au revoir. Oh typical, my carriage 18 is miles away. Without time to take my coat off, the sweat is running down my back.

Finally reaching my carriage, the ticket attendant casts a cursory glance over my ticket, "Oui, oui Madame, vite vite." He is more worried that the train leave on time than checking my ticket.

"Pardon, pardon", squeezing down the aisle between the seats already crowded with excess luggage. Lurching from seat to seat as SNCF 5222 glides out of Paris headed for Bordeaux St Jean.

Phew I made it. The seating numbers are covered in a sea of woolly scarves, finally Seat 52. Shoving my coat and hat into the overhead rack and feeling like a train wreck. I plomp down beside a petite French lady, glancing over her chic red glasses she smiles and returns to her novel. Well, at least she looks friendly, so I will attempt a little French conversation closer to my destination. Pulling my new black skivvy under my bottom, stopping it rolling up over my tummy, I am not feeling very chic. A stray curl flicks over my eyes and I pull it back down behind my ear. Maria thinks I should try to grow my hair, so I am giving it a go. If it looks too much like a poodle I will have a very French haircut.

"SNCF Welcomes you aboard 5222, destination Bordeaux St Jean. We hope you enjoy your journey. Our restaurant carriage is open for your pleasure. Express to Tours, change at Poitiers for Limoges."

The announcement was broadcast in French, but to my relief is flashing up in English over the carriage doorway. Nursing my bag on my lap I can feel my eyelids getting heavy.

Not feeling like Joan of Arc's bootlace, desperate to catch up on some sleep after my early start, I set my tiny travel clock for midday, enough time for a little visit to the restaurant car for *un petit verre du vin blanc*. As luck would have it the bar is only one carriage away, not too far to navigate over bags and backpacks.

Pointing to the red wine, the waiter has not understood me. I try again, "Juste un verre de vin rouge merci," thinking I sounded very French, I don't know what his problem is.

Heaving myself up onto the high back chair at the narrow bar while the train buzzes along at 200 kph is no easy feat. French people beside me look completely at ease, standing sipping their very hot black coffee, gently breaking croissants without leaving a crumb.

Tiny villages with church spires poking out, misty hills, trees revealing mistletoe nests. Scenery like a moving painting more beautiful than I imagined. Slowly letting the frenetic morning ebb away. My Cote Du Rhone plastic cup of red wine is lulling me to a happy place.

Maria was right, "Find your feet Izzy, cities are cities, but the heart of Europe is in the countryside."

I have never been a summer person. Autumn and spring are my favourite seasons. Arriving to a French misty fall will be my heaven.

With just forty minutes till we arrive in Poitier and feeling much more relaxed than this morning, I make my way back along the aisle to seat 52.

The next bit should be easy, small station, down the ramp to the local Platform 43, plenty of time. I have will have fifteen minutes to get onto the local train.

Slowing down the train comes to a halt. Surrounded by green rolling fields not a house to be seen, let alone a medieval city like Poitier.

Hmmm, hoping they are just waiting for a train to pass I try to stay calm. There is now only 20 minutes till my connection leaves Poitiers for Montmorillon.

Smiling at the lady beside me I glance at my watch. She doesn't return my smile "Ce n'est pas bon," she says tapping her watch. Oh Mon Dieu.

Gathering she is not happy, I attempt to ask what's happening?

"Ah pardon Madame, pourquoi we stopping?"

"Désolé, je ne parle pas anglais," she apologises politely, Oh god, how can I find out what's happening?

Flashing overhead messages, answer my question, enough for even me to realise there is a problem.

"Ce train arrivera dix minutes plus tard à Poitiers." The train is running ten minutes late. Oh shite. At this rate I will miss my connecting train.

The train lurches forward, at least we are moving. The lady beside me smiles a knowing smile. Minutes tick past and we are stopped again.

There is a growing number of people jumping up and pulling down cases from the overhead rack. Balancing with hats in one hand and cases at the ready. Looks of concern and hushed speech between passengers waiting to leap off. This does not look good. The aisle is already filling up with bags and people anxious to make a quick exit, it's going to take me five minutes just to disembark.

Its midday as we crawl into Poitiers station, I have just four minutes to clamber off this train and race to my Montmorillon connection. They will hold the next train surely? Starting to regret the decision to travel alone and wishing I could confer with somebody, anybody.

Finally, it's my turn to leap off the train, belting along the platform, oh fuck. I look up and there are at least twenty stairs climbing up to the overpass. Pardon, pardon. Here I go again, heart attack number two.

Racing into the foyer looking up to the departures,

Limoges via Montmorillon and Le Dorat platform 43, looking around through the sea of people for a sign I spot the arrow towards 43 beside the Paul's Boulangerie.

With my hat and scarf tucked firmly under my arm, I run through to an empty platform. Not a train in sight.

The station attendant yells to me and points down the long platform. Sitting at the end in the distance is a two-carriage train, looking like a toy compared to the Montparnasse loco I have just disembarked from.

Wishing I had lost more weight before I left, I start to jog towards the train. Please don't go, please don't go.

Whistling its departure, the Montmorillon connection pulls away without me on board.

With my breath burning my lungs, I turn around and walk slowly back to the Poitiers station foyer. All my life I have wanted to make my own decisions, travel to the beat of my own drum. Maybe I should be careful what I wish for. Feeling defeated I drag my little case over the stones towards the ticket information.

"Pardon, Monsieur, my train was late so I have missed my Montmorillon train."

Thinking part French and part English will do the trick.

I am met with a blank stare through the glass screen.

Try again.

"Je suis désolé, je parle petit français, vous parlez anglais?"
Very happy with myself I give him a little smile.
"I try speak little English with you," he chuckles
"Oh merci," I smile at him gratefully.
"There one more train to Montmorillon, it leave 18:00."
"Really?" Glancing at my watch. That's four hours away.
Accepting defeat I shrug my shoulders,
"Merci, Monsieur."
Turning towards the waiting room I hear him shout.
"Ah, Madame," he points to the taxi sign over the exit.

Thinking anything is worth a try I wander through to the taxi rank. Just a 40-minute train trip to Montmorillon surely a taxi wouldn't cost much? Maybe divine intervention, it will be easier this way. The driver can take me straight to the local hotel.

Just one taxi sitting waiting in the queue. Great, what luck, last car.

I lean towards the half open window,

"Bonjour Monsieur, c'est combien pour Montmorillon?" Hoping to sound very French and not get ripped off as a tourist.

"Montmorillon?" he says, as though he has never heard of it. "100 euros."

In shock, I don't even try to think of the French. "What, you are joking. 100 euros?"

"Oui, Madame, it is 40 Kilometres."

"No, thank you." Despondent, I walk back into the station. This is going to be a long wait. Planning to get to Montmorillon before dark, settle into my hotel, look at some maps, nice dinner in the restaurant. Ah well, I would arrive in the dark about 7pm so still time for a delicious French meal and plenty of time to explore tomorrow.

Thinking of my Wheel of Fortune and still hoping it is not deserting me.

Exhausted from all that the day has thrown at me and

settling into the waiting room, I let my book transport me to medieval France.

Not fully believing I am 12,000 kilometres from home, almost to Montmorillon.

Simone De Beauvoir's Grave, Montparnasse Cemetery

Chapter 10

Montmorillon station sits in darkness except for one little light above the exit gate.

Only two other people hopped off the train arm in arm, they head towards the only car in the car park. It seems so dark and lonely. There is no taxi rank and nobody to be seen. After the noise of Paris its seems deathly quiet here and it's only just after 7pm.

My Lonely Planet guide says it's an easy 15-minute walk into town, I had intended to arrive in daylight. Damn missing my connecting train. The autumn chill in the air brushes against my skin, so pulling my hood up over my scarf and taking a deep breath I head down the pathway towards the street lights glowing in the distance.

The station is next to two large silos connected to old buildings, they look like they have come from a World War 2 movie set, its eerie, I can imagine a large Nazi flag draped around them, cattle trucks filled with French Jews being sent to the camps.

Shivering and trying to think of happier things, I hope not long till I will be in a nice hot bath, followed by dinner. Not having anything to eat since I arrived at Poitier station, butterflies in my stomach are growling to be fed.

There was only one place to stay listed in Montmorillon Centre Ville, "Hotel De France", 24 rooms, bistro and restaurant. Other accommodation was in surrounding villages or on the outskirts of town.

Taking a chance and not booking, as it's not the busy summer season, taking my travels agents' advice, not tying myself to pre-arrangements.

"You will probably fall in love with Paris and want to stay longer than three nights, Izzy," she had said.

I did fall in love with Montparnasse, but scared that if I stayed too long, I would chicken out and not follow my plans to find Bella's friend.

Walking down the road towards the light, things seem brighter. Shuttered stone houses shining their warmth from old chandeliers. Families gathering around tables, oblivious to the passing commuters, the scent of freshly baked bread getting stronger with every step.

Lonely Planet, my travel bible says Montmorillon is spread over two sides of a valley. The Gartempe River meandering through its centre, the ancient bridge built in 1407, connecting the 11th century medieval town to the more recent 18th century buildings on the other. Fairly confident that the hotel will be in the newer part of town, I take a right turn at the lights and follow the Centre Ville sign. Antique lanterns light up a bridge ahead, showing off pretty flower baskets overflowing with colour. Boulangeries, still busy serving people on their way home for dinner. The whole street smells delicious.

It's been such a long day, but halfway over the bridge crossing the Gartempe I am rewarded with the most breath-taking sight. There in the distance on the bend of the river sits the medieval Cité. Towering and majestic, glowing in the early moonlight, my heart skips a beat, this makes all my trepidation worthwhile. Just over the bridge a tiny bar "La Commerce" snuggles in beside my hotel. It will be great to have a little French bar so close.

The high neon sign flashes "Hotel De France," but the front of the building is in darkness.

The sign over the glass front door says, "Fermé pour reconstruction, ouvré Novembre 30." Fuck, fuck; fuck. What am I going to do now? The hotel is closed for the next six weeks. Deciding to continue along what appears to be the high street, I pass the Cinema Majestic and La Cocotte café, both are closed. What is it with this place it's not even 7.30 and nothing is open. Ahead seems nothing more than the post office and Credit Agricole bank, so I take a left back towards the old town. Dragging my case over the cobblestones and hoping the wheels don't come off.

Relief floods through me. Ahead I can see another place to stay Hotel de Ville. Yay... my luck is in, funny that Lonely Planet didn't know about this place. It looks so pretty, adorned with little flower baskets and well-kept gardens, lit up like a Xmas tree, this looks more promising.

Walking up the concrete ramp my joy turns to concern, signs all over the front announcing upcoming events, directions for Services Publics and Aides Sociales, Horaire de la mairie. How stupid am I, it's the bloody town hall.

Continuing past the Hotel de Ville brings me to Rue De Ernest Mallier, championne de la resistance, each street or laneway has a tiny written memento that this area was a resistance stronghold in WW2.

Through large windows ahead there is a beautiful lady dressed in a turquoise sari, floating between the tables.

Yes, this is looking promising, the aroma of korma and frites wafts towards me.

Hoping I am not seeing a mirage in my exhaustion and hunger, I almost run towards the Pakistani restaurant. Just as I reach the door the turquoise lady flips over a sign: "Desolé Fermé," sorry closed.

All day I have been holding back tears, now they come dripping out of me. Too tired to be strong anymore, I choke back a little sob. Sitting on the steps outside the tourist info office blowing into a tissue, berating myself for not thinking to book ahead. Its only day four of my adventure and my new-found confidence is slipping away.

Not happy about the idea of sleeping in a doorway, I push myself to walk a little more towards the old cite. Rue de Pont Vieux leads the way to the old bridge, sitting in darkness only the stone church across the river lights the way.

One doorway throws a soft light making a beam across the dark cobblestones.

Please angels let somebody be there, I whisper.

"La Terrasse, Salon De Thé" still have their overhead light switched on, one last hope. Peeping in through the open door the inside glows, warm and inviting, plush comfy sofas, little tables covered in checked cloths, it's empty, but I can see somebody moving behind the bar piled high with teapots and glasses.

Hunger and tiredness overtake my fear of speaking French and being understood.

"Pardon, ah pardon," trying to raise my voice over the clatter of dishes in the sink and music.

Not wanting to be rude if they are closed, I stay waiting in the doorway.

Singing along to "Bohemian Rhapsody," the woman does not even notice me.

Coughing seems to attract her attention.

"Pardon Madame, je suis désolé est vous ouvré?" I try my best French. The little blond head lifts up from the dishes surprised to see somebody in her doorway.

"Sorry, love, we're closed, it's just been so busy in here today, I'm still doing the dishes. I should have shut that door ten minutes ago."

Relief to hear English spoken, but shattered they are closed, my emotions give way again. Standing fixed to the spot feeling defeated. Moving around the bar the petite lady moves towards me, looking at my case. "Are you staying in Montmorillon, then?"

Hiccuping back a sob, all I can do is nod at her.

Wiping my hand over my tears and runny nose.

"Oh, you poor thing, here sit down for a minute," she pats on the velvet sofa. "Looks like you need a drink, been a bad day then, love?" Kindness from a stranger just turns me into a sobbing machine.

She walks behind me, closing the front door, pulling over the curtains. Lifting the "Fermé, closed" stand out of her way, she totters back behind the bar. I am surprised she can walk on her four-inch heels. My head is thumping, all I can do is try to stifle my sobs, as she pours wine from a box into a glass bottle. Carrying back two glasses she sets them onto the table.

Looking up at the dishes she says, "You know, it's been a hell of a day today I could do with a break. My name's Kim, this is my tearoom, what's your name then, love?" she asks me kindly.

"Izzy," I mumble feeling like a four-year old who has lost their mother shopping, slowly I recount my day to her. Running for trains, missing my connection, nowhere to stay. Feeling like a failed tourist.

Kim laughs out loud when I say I thought the Hotel de Ville was a hotel.

"Don't worry love, if I had a euro for everybody I know that's done that, I'd be a wealthy woman."

"Really?" I return her smile. It's warm and comforting here, the wine is working its magic. "My mother passed away only two months ago, it's been such an emotional time, I'm sorry, I'm not usually a cry baby."

Kim pats my hand gently, "Look, Izzy, I have a tiny gîte out the back, it's not much but there is a comfy bed sofa and a little kitchenette, I just keep it for friends coming over, you are welcome to stay for a couple of nights and we can have a big chat tomorrow and work out a plan."

I hesitate to reply, reading my mind she cuts in, "I live upstairs here, so you won't be in my way. Tomorrow is my day off, I have a well-deserved sleep in, I run this place on my own so by the time Monday comes around I don't do a thing. You won't be able to sort anything else tonight." Not waiting for an answer she takes my hand.

"Come on, it's this way." She leads me, out of the back door and down the stairs, outside through a side door, into the laneway behind the building, up another set of stairs onto a terrace. There is a small cottage looking out over a large seating area, just a stone wall separating it from the river. Chairs and tables are stacked under tarpaulins and a huge knobbly grape vine is winding its way along the side stone walls. Towering over us is the church I saw before.

"Oh wow, it's beautiful," I say, gasping.

"It is beautiful in the summer, but it's a mess now," she waves her hand pointing to all the fallen leaves. "It's closed now till next spring, so you arrived at a good time. I can't let anybody stay here in the summer because the terrace is too busy with customers."

Kim turns the key, pushing open the door and switching on the light. "It's nothing special, but you are welcome to it for a few days if it helps, sorry it's a bit musty," she says wrinkling up her nose. "Just about everything is closed here on a Monday so I will pop some teacakes into you in the morning and we can have a cuppa."

DONG DONG DONG—bells ring out and I almost jump into Kim's arms. She laughs. "You'll get used to those, thank God they stop at 11pm, see you tomorrow, love, sweet dreams." Kim closes the door and leaves me. Throwing my scarf and hat onto the floor not even bothering to undress, I collapse on the sofa and pull the eiderdown around me.

Gartempe river, Notre Dame & Cité de L'Ecrit, Montmorillon

Chapter 11

Waking after a fantastic sleep, I climb up the tiny staircase where upstairs is a sweet little dressing and shower room. The windows look out over the terrace to the old bridge and medieval church tower. The sky is the bluest I have ever seen, across the river the row of little stone maisons are glowing in the sunlight. Butterflies in my stomach are fluttering with excitement, maybe today, with Kim's help I can find my aunt's friend Sophie.

There is a tap on the glass door and running downstairs I find Kim balancing a tray with two steaming mugs of coffee and a plate of buttery teacakes. Sitting them down on an old chest she smiles, "There you go, you must be starving. I know it's not croissants, our closest boulangerie is closed on Mondays, there is a great one further up the hill, but I am too lazy. I make all the cakes myself."

Her friendly chatter puts me at ease. Not believing my luck at finding this angel.

"I am not allowed to bake French cakes only English cakes, can you believe that?" she chatters on, I am not sure if she expects an answer, without pausing for breath she explains that you have to be a trained boulanger or patissier to open a coffee shop and sell homemade French gateaux and croissants. "It's to protect the skills of the artisans."

"Well, it sounds fair to me," I add, thinking I had better contribute to the conversation while Kim takes a pause.

"So I opened an English tea shop with scones and chocolate cake. The French people loved it, something different, pots of tea, scones with jam and cream. That was five years ago."

Reaching over for my second teacake I'm taking in her story. "Thanks Kim, these are amazing."

"Oh, they're my mum's recipe, she's a great cook. Did you sleep OK, Izzy?"

"I think I was asleep before my head hit the cushion, I

didn't even make it up to the bedroom," I laugh.

"Are you planning on staying in Monty long?" she asks.

I smile at her term of endearment for the town.

"Really I have not a clue," I answer with my mouth full of teacake. "I love all the history in these little French towns, my aunt used to live here."

"Really, where is she now?" Kim looks intrigued.

"Sadly, she died five years ago of ovarian cancer."

"Oh, that's so sad, did you ever get to meet her?"

"No, my mother moved to Australia from London, she never saw her family again. I'm an only child, now that my mum has passed away, it's just me, on my own."

We finish the coffee and teacakes in silence.

Kim looks thoughtful but doesn't say anything.

I decide to ask for her help.

"Kim, I don't know if you can help me, but I have an address for a friend of my aunt's. It's all I have, that and her name. I am hoping she still lives in Montmorillon and might be able to tell me a little about my aunt. I never even knew my grandparents, now I am on my own it would mean so much to find out a bit more about my family. If I can't find her I will just rest a few days here then take the train down to Bordeaux. I don't really have any plans, for the first time in my life, I can do what I like." Wanting to feel excited, but sick with nerves.

Kim doesn't seem fazed by my crazy excuse for being in Montmorillon. Maybe she senses my need for reassurance.

Reaching over to my bag I unzip the side pocket.

"This is all I have," I say, handing Bella's letter to Kim. She pulls her glasses down onto her little nose. She could almost be French with her elfin features and chic short haircut. I feel so frumpy and fat sitting beside her.

"Well what a sad letter, I'm sorry, love, I don't remember your aunt, but I think the name of her friend sounds familiar.

Have you got any idea what age she might be?" Kim looks thoughtful.

"Well, all I know is my Aunt Bella was twenty years younger than my mother, so she would have been about fifty. I have no idea about Bella's friend Sophie, other than her address," I say, looking hopefully at Kim.

"It's around the time I decided to start up a business here, making this my home. You are in luck, though, Rue Puits Cornet is just over the bridge down along the river. Do you want to meet up this afternoon? I just have a few bills to pay at the La Poste and a gift to send, my day is free after that, we can go for a wander, I will show you around the town. Maybe we can find your aunt's friend, if not, I know lots of people in town who can help us."

Not believing my good luck at finding such a kind helpful person, I say a quiet thank you to my Dad. Maybe he is watching over me. My Wheel of Fortune hasn't deserted me after all.

"If you're sure Kim, I really don't want to take up your time on your day off, you have already been so kind."

"It's no trouble love, I go for a walk every day," she pats her non-existing stomach, which makes me feel even more overweight.

"Not much is open on Mondays, so I can make us a sandwich before we head off."

Agreeing to meet at midday, Kim heads back across the terrace, leaving me on my own, with my thoughts.

Elated, I start a letter to Maria and Joe, hoping to finish later with the good news that I have found Sophie Le Foy.

After a delicious cheese toastie Kim locks the front of La Terrace, we walk down Rue de Pont Vieux and back out over the square. Everything looks so much cheerier in the daylight, my despair of the night before seems a distant memory. Fountains in front of the tourist info are switched off so we take the short cut across and walk around the front of the mairie. Even in the daylight the town hall looks more like a pretty hotel than council offices.

The town seems like a ghost town, Kim assures me that most businesses have the day off on Mondays.

"You wait till tomorrow, it will be buzzing, in the summer everybody sits outside in the sun drinking beer and wine. They have lots of concerts here in the square, everybody dances, its great fun."

She talks as if I will still be here in the summer. Hoping she knows something that I don't, I already have a good feeling about this little town.

Pushing open the doors to La Poste we see there are already a few people in the queue.

Kim sighs, "You'll get used to this, nobody is in a hurry and everybody has a chat with the post lady."

It seems so old fashioned and yet so pleasing, people taking time to connect with each other like they used to at home years ago. None of the people in the line seem bothered, each knowing they will have their turn for a chat.

"Bonjour Madame. Je voudrais envoyer cette boîte à l'Angleterre." She slides the parcel over the counter, whispering to me, "It's a parcel for my mum's birthday."

I hope one day I will sound as French as Kim does.

"Il fait soleil," the post lady says, more interested in commenting on the weather than weighing the parcel.

"It's their favourite conversation—they're obsessed about the weather," Kim laughs.

"Au revoir, a bientôt."

Everybody is so polite.

Kim leads us back across the square, up past La Terrasse and over the old bridge. Halfway across we stop to admire La Gartempe River, winding its way through Montmorillon. The vista is like a painting, water so clear I can see the trout swimming along. Kim points out some of the impressive buildings sitting proudly on the banks of the river.

"That's the old Palais de Justice, it's a chambre d'hôte now, it's just been renovated."

I follow her finger to a medieval tower on the right, jutting out over the river.

We walk over the bridge, which dates back to 1407, past Le Roman des Saveurs, a restaurant with a fabulous outlook over the river. Ahead of us is a winding pedestrian cobblestone street leading up into the medieval Cité de L'Ecrit.

"Wow," I let out an exclamation, "It's just so pretty."

"It's magical," Kim replies, "especially when the sun is shining. We sit out here overlooking the river, from April they bring out the tables and chairs."

I can see myself here, drinking wine in the sun, starting to understand why my Aunt Bella might have settled here.

Instead of climbing up into the medieval city, we take a right turn, down beside the river. Rue Puits Cornet. Skipping a little beat, my heart is pumping fast, I can't believe I am so close to finding Bella's friend.

Please, please be home I think to myself.

Rue Puits Cornet is a quaint country laneway, leading behind several cafes and out beside the river. The first few houses sit in the shadow of the Notre Dame Church, they have views back across the river to the town.

"How lucky are the people that live here, the views are so pretty."

Kim senses my excitement. "I guess you don't have many medieval churches in Australia?"

We pick our way carefully over the cobblestones, Kim in her three-inch heels, me in my sensible trainers. I could stop and take photos of every doorway, moss covered stone archways leading to secret river gardens. Maria and Joe's parting gift to me, a Nokia camera, is going to be well used.

Kim says there are lots of tunnels under Montmorillon, dating back over a thousand years. It's like I am in a dream, but I try to stay in the moment, at any minute I might meet Madame Le Foy.

On both sides of the lane there are gardens enclosed in high stone fences. Stretching up and peeping over into some of them, I can see, well maintained rows of vegetables and fruit trees. Many have little cabins built into the side of the cliff.

"The French love their vegetable gardens, all the neighbours swap veggies and fruit, everybody makes jam." Pretty shuttered villas start up again on the cliff side of the laneway, each outdoing the other with flowering window boxes.

"You wait till the spring, Izzy, its stunning along here."

No 32 has a massive garden to the side and huge green solid gates. A padlock and chain is drawn across the front and there is no doorbell. From the laneway we can see trees growing out of the side of the cliff, there is a ledge with a little cabin painted pink that appears to be separated from ground floor building. The house looks more like a garage. Feeling my heart sinking I wait for Kim to catch up.

"What do you think?" should we bang on the gate?" I ask.

Kim shrugs her shoulders. "It's not very welcoming looking is it? I don't know any expats living down here, it's all old French families, they have had these gardens for years." Kim doesn't sound very hopeful.

Undeterred, I decide to give a shout, "Bonjour bonjour! Anybody home?" We hear a rustle through the bushes, behind the gates and a loud grrrrrrr woooof wooof.

Jumping back from the gate, not expecting there would be a dog. Through a tiny slit where the gates meet I can see shiny brown eyes and a golden coat.

"Hello fella, what's your name?" He seems very friendly, wagging his tail.

"Maybe your aunt's friend is at work?" Kim is trying to give me some hope. After a few minutes there is still no sign of human life, we decide to walk further along the river.

Finding nobody at home my mood has rapidly declined. Kim is trying her best to cheer me up.

"Let's go up into the medieval town for a beer, tomorrow I will take you to meet my friend Hero, she's an English real estate agent on the square. She's worked and lived in Monty for over twenty years and even if she doesn't know your aunt's friend she's bound to know somebody that does."

Not as good as I hoped for, it's still a lovely plan and not wanting to ruin Kim's day off, I smile at her and agree.

"You're right, tomorrow is another day, there's no hurry, at least we know somebody lives there."

Kim adds, "Hero pops in on a Tuesday evening for an apéro just before I close up, I will introduce you and am sure she will be happy to chat with you."

"What's an apéro?" I reply.

Kim laughs, "It's a French way of life, they love to get together with friends for a drink before dinner, it's usually Kir Royale, bubbles with cassis."

"I could get used to this, what a lovely tradition," I laugh back.

Linking her arm through mine we head up the hill, "Come on, let's go for that beer, you're in for a treat. *La Trappe aux Livres* has over 70 beers."

"Guessing they don't have Fosters?" I laugh.

"You will never drink Aussie beer again once you try Belgian Beer," she replies.

Kim's cheeriness lifts my spirits, even though Sophie Le Foy has not been home I am feeling happier than I have in years.

Sitting in the autumn sun sipping our large Affligems, Kim and I both share snippets of ourselves. She is on her own with no siblings and very elderly parents who still live in the UK. Behind her bubbly, sunny personality she worries about being alone. Her story of setting up the tea shop with no

French and doing all the renovations herself is inspiring. What a courageous woman.

In many ways we are very similar, and it seems I have found a lovely new friend.

Aperos, Place Du Maréchal Le Clerc, Montmorillon

Chapter 12

Kim was right, Montmorillon is much buzzier on Tuesdays.

Today the square is full of cars, all the shops have their shutters open, and people are going about their daily tasks. I have all day to fill in before meeting Kim's friend for apéros at 5pm, in the La Terrasse tea room.

After a few hours browsing, I decide to cross back over the old bridge to the other side of town, past the St Martial Eglise. Locals are playing petanque on the Place de Victoire, another pretty square. There are so many tired-looking, shuttered houses with *A Vendre*, "For Sale" signs, it starts me thinking, what it would be like to live in this friendly little town. Having no idea of the cost of French rural real estate, I assume it's out of my price range.

As usual, I am dreaming, getting ahead of myself. First things first: tonight I am hoping that Kim's friend Hero can put me in touch with Madame Le Foy.

The Red Cross charity shop sits overlooking the square. Already bored with the three outfits I squeezed into my carry-on luggage, I pop in to see if I can find a bargain. Kim said all her clothes come from the charity shops. Hard to believe as she is so elegantly dressed. French women seem tiny to me, and I can't believe they eat so much bread and cheese. They believe that eating proper meals and no snacking in between is the key to a healthy lifestyle. There are no takeaway shops in Montmorillon unless you count the Pizza Bella on the square, even that has little tables and chairs so you can sit and enjoy a glass of vin rouge with your crispy base pizza, smothered in lashings of French cheese and homemade salami. Trying to stick to small portions is not going to be easy.

Doubting I will find anything to fit me, I smile at the volunteers working on the cash register. "Bonjour Madame," they say in unison, pointing the way down the hallway to the ladies clothing room.

Everything is perfectly separated into sizes, its only seconds before I spot a beautiful green velvet jacket, some leather pumps and a checked shift dress.

"Merci Madame," the sales lady smiles as she takes my 10 euro note, handing me two euros change. What a bargain, this lot would have cost me a fortune in Melbourne. Very happy with my purchases I wish them "*à* bientôt," I will certainly be back before I leave.

Passing St Martial on my way back, the bells ring out four times. Heading back to Kim's gîte I know there will just be time for a siesta, and freshen up, before apéros and my meeting with Hero.

After a snooze and quick shower, pulling my new shift over my black skivvy, my reflection surprises me.

More like my forty-year old self and less like my seventy-year old mother.

My hair has changed, slightly longer, with hints of copper showing through the last remnants of the "L'oreal Inky," hair dye, still growing out. Black tights with added stomach control, add to the illusion, I am starting to look slimmer. Slipping into my new shoes I feel somehow lighter and ready to enjoy myself. Walking every day, eating healthy food, even my fingernails are starting to grow.

Just a little spray of Issey Miyake, my favourite scent, a duty free pressie to myself.

Silly to feel nervous about meeting Kim's friends, but I really want to make a good first impression. Kim has said I can stay in the gîte as long as I need, in exchange for helping on the busy tea room days. Wednesdays are market days, the tearoom opens at 10am, I will help to clear tables, hopefully improving my French speaking with the local French women.

Everything seems to be slipping into place. It's such a

friendly town, my money will last longer if I don't have to pay for accommodation for a while.

Nearly dark outside, walking down the steps from the gîte, the warm glow of La Terrace is so welcoming. Kim is a tiny little thing, feeling the cold, she always has the heating cranked up to the max. Pushing open the door, I pat my tummy to quieten my butterflies. Meeting new people is not my favourite thing, I wish I didn't feel so nervous.

Sitting behind the bar, perched on a stool laughing and enjoying the company of her friends, Kim looks very relaxed. Two blonde haired ladies sit opposite her, their legs crossed elegantly, another leans across the bar sipping a glass of bubbles. They all turn and watch me as I walk past the sofas to join them.

"Izzy," Kim greets me warmly. "Come and meet everybody." She pops out from behind the bar, guiding me around the chatty group.

"This is Hero, my friend who runs a real estate agency on the square." Hero has an infectious smile, holding out her hand to me.

"Welcome Izzy, Kim tells me that you're staying in the gîte and might stay for a while?"

Kim interrupts, "This is Jane." The dark-haired pretty girl steps forward.

"Hi ya, welcome to Monty."

"This is Pat."

"Welcome to our little town, Izzy," Pat rubs my arm, making me feel instantly at ease with Kim's friends.

"We're all having Kir Royales," Kim says, tottering back around the bar. "It's cassis blackcurrant liquor in bubbles. Can I get you one?"

"Yes please, sounds delicious," thinking I really need a drink to help calm my nerves.

The girls pull a stool in between them, I climb up, realising my new shift is too tight for me to cross my legs. Still lots of work to be done in the exercise department. Glad now I made the effort to dress up, but regretting my choice of such a tight dress. The girls look so glamorous.

Everybody chatters on, asking me questions and time passes effortlessly. Hero hasn't mentioned my aunt, I am wondering if Kim has even told her about my search...

Pat is Hero's mother, she looks so young, it's hard to believe. All these girls have beautiful skin. The harsh Australian sun has really aged my skin, I feel as though I look older than all of them. Hero is tall, elegant with bouncy blonde curls, and a very pretty face. Jane has dark wavy hair and is wearing the most amazing shirt. When I compliment her on the fabric, she points across the laneway to her shop La Petite Mercerie.

"Jane makes the most amazing bespoke bags," quips Hero.

"Everybody wishes they can sew after they see Jane's fabrics."

Jane smiles at me. "Pop in and see me anytime, Izzy, I will be open tomorrow till Saturday, we are neighbours."

"Better wrap things up ladies," Kim pipes up, "I have my guitar lesson tonight."

Everybody climbs off their stools, I am disappointed that I haven't had the courage to ask Hero about Madame Le Foy.

The girls all kiss each other à bientôt, waving as they step out the door.

Hero turns and comes back to me, "Izzy why don't you pop into the office tomorrow to see me, we can chat about Madame Le Foy." I realise then she hadn't wanted to say anything in front of the others.

"Oh; thanks Hero, how is 10.30 in the morning?"

"You had better make it 11," she laughs: "I'm always running late in the mornings."

"Oh, thank you, see you at 11 then," I reply, giving her a little wave.

Hero closes the door and everything is quiet, leaving just

Kim and I washing the dishes.

"What a lovely group of friends you have, Kim, thanks for making me feel so welcome. You know, I felt really nervous about meeting everybody, but I needn't have been."

After a lifetime of feeling I don't fit in, I can't believe how in such a short time, I feel so comfortable here. Tomorrow can't come quick enough, maybe I will be a step closer to learning more about Aunt Bella.

La Petite Mercerie

Chapter 13

C/o La Terrace
Montmorillon.

Dearest Maria,
So sorry that this letter has taken me over two weeks to write. I have thought of you often and started to write to you in my head. It's a good sign I suppose that the past two weeks have just flown by.

After my long flight and first days in Montparnasse, I am now staying in Montmorillon. You were right, the people in the country are so friendly. After a few hiccups with accommodation I have been lucky enough to stay in a sweet little furnished gîte, in return for helping out in the landlady's tea shop or Salon de The, as they say here. I insisted on also paying for the electricity, but this way my funds will go much further.

How to describe Montmorillon? It's a really pretty town, surrounded by green fields and forests. There is a beautiful meandering river called La Gartempe, my gîte looks out over it to the Medieval Cité de L'Ecrit. The old cité is full of bookshops and curios to do with writing. An ancient bridge crosses to the centre of the town which makes it feel more like a village.

I was misguided to think it would be easy to find Sophie Le Foy. So far, Madame Le Foy appears to have either, left 32 Rue Puits Cornet or be out each time I try to make contact. There is a dog on the property though which helps me not to lose hope. I have also made contact with Madame Hero, a local Immobilier (Real Estate Agent), who has asked my permission to speak to the local Notaire. A Notaire is a legal specialist who looks after legal matters, he or she is appointed by the government. Each town has several Notaires so he may have information about the address and be able to help me track down Sophie Le Foy. Everything is so private here, I have to be careful not to upset anybody. Seems a lot of hoo-

hah just to find the friend of my aunt.

Maria, my Wheel of Fortune has brought me so much luck.

To find myself in this sweet town having already met so many people is unbelievable.

I can stay in the tearoom gîte till summer if I want to so am thinking it's a good omen, I will have to be patient.

Walking every day, discovering so much history in these tiny laneways is heaven. Tomorrow I will get the key for the crypt of Notre Dame Eglise and go to look at the frescoes of St Catherine who was martyred after being tortured, she broke the stretching wheel and hence the name "The Catherine Wheel." Oh, Maria you would love it here!

Every morning after my walk I pop around to the little supermarché, run by Claude and Brigitte, they don't speak a word of English so it's really helping my French. There is only a tiny bar fridge in the gîte so I am buying supplies daily. The weekly market on Wednesday mornings is an assault on my senses, full of locally grown produce, big wheels of salted butter, cheeses that I can barely pronounce. It's like a movie with accordion players and flower stalls. You will just have to come and see it for yourself.

As soon as I have more news I will write again, just hoping that my next letter will convey I have finally found Sophie Le Foy.

Hugs to Joe and love you both,

Izzy

Ps I stopped chewing my nails and my hair is nearly over my collar.

Chapter 14

Each morning I take a different direction, at some point, always passing by 32 Rue Puits Cornet, hoping still to catch Sophie on her way to work, or out to walk the dog. She seems to be the invisible woman, I can't help feeling she is possibly avoiding me. Assuming she received my letter, I can't understand her reluctance to meet me.

Today I have no plans, till this afternoon when I meet up with Hero, finally I think she may have some news for me, from the Notaire about Sophie.

Clouds are gathering as I quicken my pace over the square, Place du Maréchal LeClerc, turning right up towards St Martial Eglise the newer 18th century church in town. There is blue sky on the horizon but black clouds are rolling in quickly blocking the sun's rays. Ducking into the "Pont de Bois Bar," I just escape the coming downpour. Still not confident about going into bars on my own, I will just have to get used to it. All the bars here sell coffee as well as alcohol, doubling as coffee shops. Although the French men all seem to have a sip of the local pineau with their black coffees. This area, the Poitou Charente, is famous for its pineau, fortified wine.

At home you would be considered an alcoholic if you needed a drink in the morning, nobody seems to blink an eye here. Doorbells clang loudly as I push open the glass door, pulling down my hood, Stefan the proprietor recognises me, smiling widely, only having met him a couple of times coming here for an apéro with Jane and Kim. Twice is enough in country France to be considered a friend. Stefan makes his way around the counter, "Ça va, Izzy?" he says as he plants a kiss on both my cheeks.

Not used to so much affection from men I hardly know I blush, my cheeks burning.

Struggling out of my jacket I nod, "Oui, ça va bien, Stefan, merci."

Kim has taught me how to answer like a local, but I still feel so embarrassed at my accent. "Un café, merci." I order my coffee, looking quickly around for a place to sit before Stefan tries to engage in conversation.

Choosing a table away from the bar, so I can watch people passing by, in the rain, while I enjoy my coffee. It's black and strong, most French people don't take milk, I am getting used to the bitter taste, leaving out the sugar.

It's also better for my waistline.

There is only one other customer, a small dark-haired man sitting up at the end of the bar, he seems to be wobbling on his stool, obviously more pineaus than coffee for him, and it's only just after 10 o'clock. To my horror he slides off the stool, coming towards me. His eyes are creepy like little slits and he is smirking at me. Looking in Stefan's direction, I am hoping he sees my look for help. I am out of luck, he is totally absorbed in a phone conversation, not paying the slightest attention to his drunken patron.

"Bonnnjourrr," he slurs, thrusting his hand out at me. Not wanting to appear rude I reply, "Bonjour Monsieur," not accepting his outstretched hand. He is not to be put off and carries on his attempt at conversation.

"Je m'appelle, ummmm, Jean-Claude Allardet." He seems pleased at remembering his own name. Oh Christ, get me out of here. I decide to take the no speak the lingo approach.

"Désolé Monsieur je parle petit français."

"Ah dommage," he says, learning his face towards me so I can smell his disgusting breath. Well it's not a shame for me, I am out of here.

Pushing back my chair I almost run to grab my jacket off the coat stand, slapping a five euro note on the counter, not waiting for my change and waving to Stefan. "A bientôt," I mutter as I pull the door behind me.

What a relief to be out in the fresh air away from that

horrible man. Walking faster than usual, wanting to put distance between me and the Pont de Bois. Before I head up the steps to the top part of town, I sneak a quick look behind me, Jean-Claude is leaning against the corner of the building smoking a cigarette watching me walk away. Not wanting to let one bad encounter ruin my day I march on trying to push him out of my mind.

Still three hours till I meet up with Hero in her office, so I head up past the Place du Victoire, walking to the outskirts of town. Villas give way to rolling fields, dotted with skeletal trees, twists of ivy hugging their trunks, little nests hanging on in the breeze. Walking here is nothing like the suburbs of home, this is enchanting and I let my mind wander, imagining myself with a dog living in this pretty town, walking every day.

Many of the ladies who pop in for a pot of tea at La Terrace work at the local SPA animal rescue centres: hundreds of older dogs are there waiting to find their forever homes. Maybe, if I decide to stay I could adopt a dog. Dad and I always wanted a dog but Harriet decided for all of us that it was too much of a responsibility.

The road heads downhill, thank goodness: my shins are killing me. Over a tiny bridge and gurgling stream which runs through a camping ground. A few caravans still closed up, sheltering under trees. Mental note to ask Hero: perhaps they take permanent residents in the caravan park? If I decide to stay here I will have to find somewhere else before the summer. Kim uses the power from the gîte to serve customers on her terrace in the busy season, so I really want to have a plan well before May.

Well past the camping ground I take a right turn, back onto the road that leads into town. Carrying on along the Gartempe River past weirs and pretty picnic areas. These houses have meandering gardens with rose covered pergolas looking onto private river views. I doubt Harriet's money will stretch to a house with a scenic river view, maybe I could lease something. Feeling guilty, I haven't thought about Harriet for weeks.

Dad feels close to me often, but Harriet seems to have moved to different realm, probably singing Hallelujahs in another universe.

Hoping good karma has brought me to Monty my imagination lets loose again, it's easy to feel what it would be like to settle into the community here. Nearly back to town, walking past the local indoor swimming-pool, if only I was a swimmer. Water makes me feel so calm, but dog paddle and breast stroke is about all I can manage, always envious of my classmates, who would win blue ribbons at the school water sports carnivals. My worst nightmares were school sports days, thank the Universe that part of my life is done. Laughter and squeals drift out of the school playground, reminding me that school is fun for most kids.

Pushing open the little gate on the terrace, I can see Kim is busy with the lunchtime crowd. How fortunate I am to have this gem of a place for a few more months. Today is my fasting day, so I grab a cuppa soup to fill me up before I see Hero.

When I walk through her office door, Hero is already chatting to a young couple. She looks up at me and smiles, "With you in a moment, Izzy, just take a seat."

Feeling tired after my walk, I am happy sitting on her sofa, looking through the booklets of *maisons à vendre*. Page after page of little townhouses for sale. Being used to the exorbitant real estate market of Melbourne, the prices in Montmorillon are a pleasant surprise. Too good to be true, pretty little villas right in the centre of town, with courtyards for as little as $50,000 euros. Having the money from Harriet I could easily buy my own little place. Having plenty left over for any renovation work, or possibly set up a little bookshop. I will need an income; Harriet's money won't last forever but if I could just subsidise it.

So caught up in my own world I don't even notice the young couple leave. "Sorry, Izzy, that couple have been very time-consuming," Hero walks over and flops onto the sofa beside me, "What a day, I try to spend as much time as possible with new people moving into Monty, but sometimes I just need a mini me," she laughs.

"I haven't had a chance to even grab lunch. Do you mind if I make a quick coffee? Can I get you one?"

I follow Hero into the tiny kitchen out the back while she boils the kettle, turning on the coffee machine. "I am impressed, real coffee," the waft of coffee beans reminds me of my unpleasant coffee experience this morning.

"I met a real moron this morning in the Pont de Bois." I relate my story to Hero. "He gave me the creeps, even after I left he followed me out and watched me walk up the hill."

"Well I guess every town has its morons," Hero laughs, "Even Montmorillon, we are pretty lucky here, the French men are generally respectful. What was his name?" she asks.

"Jean-Claude," I say with a frown on my face.

"Just keep away from him, Izzy. He's harmless but gives all the new ladies in town a run for their money. He is an alcoholic who doesn't work, he comes from a very wealthy Montmorillonais family, he thinks he's God's gift to women. His parents died in a car accident when he was young, raised by his grandparents, he is spoilt brat, a man who is still indulged by his family and behaves like a child." Hero gives me a warning look.

"I guess it can't have been easy losing his parents so young," I remark, "but still no excuse for being a sleaze bucket."

Hero laughs again. "Your Ozzie sayings are hilarious, Izzy, you have cheered me up."

She leads the way back to her desk, covered in piles of

paperwork. "This is this afternoon's work," she sighs.

Feeling guilty for asking Hero to help me find Sophie, I wish I could wave my magic wand and take it all away.

Not wanting to seem too pushy I wait while she takes a long sip of her coffee.

"Sorry, it's taken me awhile to get back to you, Izzy, but I had to wait for the Notaire to get back from a funeral in Paris."

"Please don't apologise, Hero, I feel bad for taking you from your work."

"It's fine, the Notaire is an old friend, we used to work together, before I set up Maisons Rurales. It's always nice to get to have a chat together."

Hero lifts up a folder behind her and flips it open.

"Well, Monsieur Dupont, the Notaire does know your aunt," she corrects herself. "I mean, did know your Aunt. Isabella Parker purchased 32 Rue Puits Cornet nearly 15 years ago. Monsieur Dupont did the contracts for completion of the sale. When she died over five years ago there was no will, she probably assumed that her partner, Sophie Le Foy, could just go on living there. In French law, you cannot leave property to somebody unless you're married or have a civil union. Without any details of her descendants, the Notaire was unable to contact anybody re inheritance." Hero pauses for breath. "As Madame Le Foy was living in the house it was agreed she could rent the property for a nominal amount, which would go to the estate monitored by the Notaire. There is foncières tax here on properties." Hero sees my vague look. "Oh, it's like council rates, a yearly tax." She continues, "That and Tax d'habitation would probably amount to about 1000 euros a year. As long as Sophie's monthly rent covered the outgoings, the Notaire was happy for her to stay. Until either somebody turns up to claim inheritance, or she can't pay the taxes, it would just go on until Madame Le Foy chose to leave. It's quite common here, people die without wills or living relatives, the houses are just locked up and left. As Bella Parker's only living relative and her niece you inherit the property." Hero pauses, looking at me, I am just too dumb struck in shock to reply.

Slowly, the words come tumbling out, "What? … ummm, are you saying that I own that house?"

"Well yes, technically you do, it will still take a few months of paperwork and transferring documents," laughing, "you know the French and paperwork, everything takes time." Hero's joke is lost on me, I am still trying to come to grips with the fact that I own that sweet little house on the river in France.

"But what about Sophie Le Foy?" I exclaim.

"Well, that would be up to you," Hero shrugs her shoulders. "Perhaps you could rent it to her, or you could sell it, or you could live there."

Suddenly a moment of clarity comes to me remembering the bit about my aunt and Sophie being partners…

"So my aunt and Madame Le Foy were living together?" I stutter.

"Yes, it would appear so," she replies, looking uncomfortable.

Hero pauses, not sure where to go with the conversation.

All I can think about is my aunt, my namesake, was living with a woman. It's nothing I mind at all, it's just so totally unexpected. I wonder if my mother ever knew… It would explain her reluctance to ever talk about my Aunt. Harriet's narrow-minded view of the world would not tolerate a lesbian sister.

"So they were lovers?"

Hero struggles to answer me. "Well I don't know if they were lovers, but they lived together for fifteen years till your aunt died of ovarian cancer. I hope you don't mind, but I have told Monsieur Duval your story, he will do everything he can to help you change the titles for the property into your name. I can help with all the translating, and there will be a fee probably around 2000 euros for all the documentation to be transferred into your name."

"That's fine, I have money, it's just such a shock," I say, shaking my head in disbelief.

"Once the property title is in your name, you can make some decisions about what you want to do."

Hero stands up, and I realise there are other clients waiting to see her.

"Izzy, I know this is a shock but it's a happy shock, yes? Why don't I meet you at Kim's after work and we can have a drink and talk through the next steps." She guides me in the direction of the door. "See you at 6.30," she calls after me, "ask Kim if she minds staying open a bit later for me."

The sun is already dipping behind the tourist info building as I walk across the square, I am shivering, I think it's from shock not from cold.

Not wanting to be on my own, I decide to wait for Hero in the tearoom. It's been weeks since I have had a drink but this afternoon I order a gin.

"Hero wants to talk to you about something, Kim, she asked can you leave the door open for her after you shut?" I cast her a quizzical look.

"You look weird, Izzy, are you ok?" Kim tilts her face at me.

"Yep, I'm fine, we'll talk when Hero gets here."

Chapter 15

The girls agree with me, Sophie Le Foy probably did receive my letter, hoping that if she ignored it nothing would eventuate.

Learning that Bella my aunt was a lesbian, living with another woman probably explains why Harriet hardly ever spoke of her sister.

Bella's final letter to my mother said she had written many times. Was it just an oversight on Harriet's part that she didn't destroy that letter as well? Accidentally finding Bella's letter has drawn me to Montmorillon, it feels like an omen. I feel as though Bella would like me to put things right. I don't need her house, thanks to Harriet and Dad I have money of my own. Poor Madame Le Foy, probably living in fear since Bella's death that one day somebody will take the house from her.

I've asked Hero to go ahead, letting the Notaire know, as soon as the title is in my name, I will have it legally transferred to Madame Le Foy. Apparently it cannot be changed directly into her name as she did not inherit it. All this paperwork probably keeps somebody in a job, but seems completely unnecessary.

None of this changes anything for me, I still desperately want to talk to Sophie Le Foy and find about the last years my aunt lived here in Montmorillon. Harriet must have been scared that just as she left her parents for a more exciting world, maybe I would do the same thing. Coming to France to meet my Aunt Bella.

I feel cheated, I didn't know I had an aunt living in France. So wishing I could just turn back time and have got to known my namesake.

Looking at my tarot cards sitting on the trunk, I decide a reading is long overdue. There is a tiny shop all boarded up a few doors up the lane, from Jane's shop. Every day I walk past it and think it would be the perfect location for an esoteric bookstore. If it has a space upstairs that I could turn into a little apartment. Butterflies in my stomach leap about thinking of a dream that long ago became shelved in my "too hard" basket.

Slowly my French is improving, thanks mostly to the patience of the "La Terrace" customers. Perhaps I could start slowly with English clients from the town and surrounding villages, giving tarot readings, slowly moving on to include basic readings for French clients.

Maybe even running a course for people who would like to learn more about the symbology of the cards.

The old shop is No 1 Rue de Vieux Pont, overlooking the river on one side, is the last doorway before the old bridge. It would make the perfect place for tarot readings, a glass of wine for tourists and locals while they browse. I would fill it with novels full of magical esoteric history, crystals and runes the tiny Egyptian stones that predate even the tarot. As always placing faith in my cards, tonight I hope they will tell me I am on the right path. It's been four months since my reading with Maria. Such a private part of me, yet to share with my new friends in Montmorillon.

I will have to tell Hero my plans for a shop, as I will need her help to search the title, seeing if it's possible for me to buy the *petit magasin*. That's if it's even for sale. Grabbing my jacket and scarf I head out into the chilly morning.

The still and cold of winter has the town in its grip now, everything seems to be turning grey. At night the Christmas lights bring the *centre ville* to life for a little while. Montmorillon is in the early buzz of "Noel."

My first Christmas in the Northern Hemisphere, without the searing heat of Melbourne. All the festive cards that I have seen growing up are coming to life. We even had a smattering of snow yesterday. So white and gentle. Perfect timing for the parade of St Nicholas, all the primary school children follow St Nicholas and his donkey, around the tiny streets, the local brass band follows in a raggle taggle way, everybody ends up outside the *mairie* for hot chocolate.

Such lovely traditions are so heart-warming, the children's cries of delight as the Christmas lights are switched on, December 7 to January 7, a month every year. Not like at home with Christmas cards and decorations in the shops in August, months before Christmas.

There will be carol singing in the square on Christmas Eve and a Christmas marché, local market of hand-made crafts for gifts. Mulled wine and local children and adults, singing and folk-dancing in the streets.

Brigitte and Claude explain to me that Christmas Eve is their big feasting time. Families all get together about 11pm for a dinner that lasts hours into the morning, seeing in Christmas. December 25th is just for resting, maybe visiting neighbours later in the day for apéros and exchanging a little gift.

I am invited to their little maison, behind the Panier Sympa Supermarché, for Christmas Eve dinner. It's going to be so special, I feel like a child all over again. Guilty that I should spend Christmas day with Kim, she assures me that she never spends Christmas day with anybody. When I mention it to her she replies quickly, "It's my day, love, to chill out and be totally slothful, I never share it with anyone."

La Terrace has moved onto winter hours, now not opening till 3pm, so my mornings are my own. My favourite walk is still over the old bridge, past the little sad shop all boarded up, that one day I hope to breathe life into. Looking up at the medieval archangel over the doorway, what stories she could tell. The rusty black cat sign is hanging from its hinges, swinging in December's breeze, blowing up from the river. They are calling to me. "Izzy, Izzy, don't give up on us." Chipped faded shutters need a coat of lilac paint. A smart new sign, "Le Petit Chat Noir," Magasin Esoteric, vin et café, bienvenu. Tarot lectures par Isabella Baker. Of course in English for all the tourists, The Little Black Cat, Esoteric Boutique, wine and coffee, all welcome.

Thinking of Dad's advice about bricks and mortar, if I could buy this little place I would have a home and an income. Oh please angels help me to make this happen.

Wrapped up in my own little happy place, I pick up my pace, over the bridge, always pausing for just a second to gaze down at the Gartempe winding its way through the town, on its journey crossing the Vienne Valley. Turning into Rue Puits Cornet and down alongside the river, I have grown so accustomed to walking past seeing the gates chained at No 32, almost not noticing that the chain is hanging off the lock, dangling in a puddle. The gate is still clipped shut, but there is no sign of my waggy tailed friend. Used to me chatting to him through the slit in the gate, passing on my daily walks, he has given up his attempt at barking like a guard dog. Pushing his wet nose through the space where the gates hang crooked, wishing I could give him a hug.

Past the stone walled gardens with their faded secrets, ahead of me stretches the laneway headed for the dog park, "Les Ilettes." It's a wide-open grassy area on the banks of the river, perfectly safe for exercising dogs off the lead, with little or no traffic. Rue Puits Cornet changes names as it turns around a bend and becomes Chemin des Ilettes, as it follows alongside the river. In the distance there is somebody approaching me, a dog bounds ahead, her voice is carried away on the wind as she tries to call back her charge.

"Ici, ici, Biscuit, ici," her cries carried away on the wind. For a minute I think the woman is calling to me "Izzy, Izzy." Then I realise she is trying to call the dog back.

Instinctively I stop in my tracks. The golden dog is flying through the air towards me, his ears flapping in the wind, oblivious to his mistress's call. Usually, I would be scared about a dog galloping towards me but something tells me this is OK, so I stand very still holding my breath.

This dog looks so much like the friendly dog behind the chained gates at No 32.

Slowing down he runs around me in circles, not growling, he seems very happy, hoping he recognises my scent from my daily chats. "Hello there boy, good boy, bonjour mon bon chien," he sits beside me tail wagging, I crouch down and pat his silky head. He is a beautiful dog with a glistening coat and brown shiny eyes.

Not quite believing I have finally met this dog from behind the gate. I look up to see a petite woman, her blond curls just escaping her hood, a pink scarf wrapped around her mouth to keep out the wind. Bundled up like an eskimo, it's hard to tell if her chilly face is just frozen with the cold or distaste at meeting me. Her pale blue eyes are almost all I can see of her face.

"Bonjour, Madame, je m'appelle Isabella Baker, enchantez," I smile and extend my hand.

She stands still, stony faced. Dropping my hand back to my side, I feel sick with a nervous stomach.

"I know who you are, you don't 'ave to tell me," she states very matter-of-factly. "I 'ave been waiting for you to come."

So not wanting to mess this up, but overjoyed that I finally get to meet Sophie, my French fails me. Ignoring her icy reception I try to keep smiling, swallowing down the lump forming in my throat.

"I see you already know Biscuit, oui?" She pats the dog on the head.

"Ah oui, il est très un bon chien, nous parlons quand je marche chaque jour." My French comes out in spits and spurts and I so hope she can understand me, I am desperate to let her see I am friendly and hope the reference to her dog will help break the ice.

Patting the dog gently, I search Sophie's face for an indication that she might be even just a little open to talking to me. Her glare cuts through me.

Without saying a word she clips the dog back onto the lead and starts to walk off. Unsure what to do, I am frozen like a statue.

Stopping, she turns around. "Well, what are you waiting for?" she calls to me. My heart is thumping and I really don't know how to respond, so I catch her up like a little girl chasing after an adult.

"I am think we have a lot of talk to do," her French accent is very endearing, I am relieved she speaks way better English than I do French.

"Yes, we do," I reply.

Christmas in Montmorillon, France. Place du Marechal Le Clerc,

Chapter 16

Reality gives way to my perception of what lays behind the chained green gates of No 32 Rue Puits Cornet. The garden is every bit as magical as I imagined. Running along the cliff wall are little walkways to cave entrances, half covered in twists of ivy and honeysuckle. The house juts out at one end of the garden, above us on a ledge sits a little cabin, pink window frames the only evidence of an attempted makeover. Hens and a regal cockerel scratch around happily in the garden beds, Biscuit the dog runs in to greet them, the chickens not paying him the slightest bit of notice. Towering over the garden a huge oak tree must provide wonderful shade in the summer, a broken old swing dangles lopsided in the breeze.

Sophie watches me quietly as my gaze takes it all in, my eyes stop at a glass conservatory sitting half covered in ivy at the bottom of the garden.

"It's my studio," she says, "I used to paint."

"Oh, what a tranquil place to paint, why did you stop?"

I look up at her hoping I haven't been too nosy.

"My subject died," she states bluntly, turning and walking towards the lean to that provides shelter over the front door. Not giving me a chance to reply Sophie kicks the bottom of the door to force it open. "It's the cold weather, everything stops working," she grumbles.

Before we go inside she picks up five logs from the stack outside the door. For a petite person she seems strong. Her pretty face showing the lines of grief, she is only just marginally taller than me. It's hard to judge her age, her blond hair has little wisps of grey just emerging around her face. Trying to imagine my mother's sister living with this woman and wishing I had been able to make the decision to come years ago. If only I had questioned Harriet more, instead of dutifully shutting up as I was expected to.

Sophie gestures for me to follow her, Biscuit pushes past me and claims his place in front of the pot belly stove. Remaining embers still glow, keeping the chill from the room.

Crooked piles of books sit on the limited bench space, a little green sofa provides the only seating. It's only lunch time but the house is dark, the skylight covered in fallen leaves, winter light too grey to brighten the room. Sophie flicks on the light over the cooker and lights a candle on the bench.

It's one long rectangular space, one end of the room is draped in heavy tapestry curtains, serving as a bedroom, behind them sits a four-poster bed. The other end of the room has a heavy sideboard, every inch covered in blue and white china. There is only one other door opposite which I assume is the toilette.

It feels very bohemian and unkempt, though cosy and comfy.

As Sophie lights more candles, the walls come alive with paintings, mostly beautiful nudes. The subject is a round-faced smiling young woman with red curls tumbling down over her breasts, posing in the garden, sitting on the swing, stretched out over the bed like a fair-skinned medieval princess. Sophie watches in silence as my eyes slowly move around the room. My heart is thumping and confusion leaves me speechless. I am sitting in a room surrounded by nudes that look like me.

"These are Aunt Bella?" both a question and a statement. Forgetting my intention to try hard to speak French, the conversation I have rehearsed for weeks has flown away."

"Yes, she was beautiful," she replies.

"There is no doubting you are her niece."

Her reference to beauty and me seems misplaced, but there is an uncanny resemblance to our round faces and red unruly hair.

116

"I remember the first day I saw her walking over the old bridge, so many years ago," her eyes glisten and I feel like I am invading such a private moment.

"All those wonderful years together, but the universe decides to take her. I like to think of her around me, her spirit still on that swing in the tree, her laughter on the wind when she rolled in the grass with Biscuit."

"Fifteen years ago she came to Montmorillon to write for *The Times* newspaper. An article about a big art festival. All the painters choose their scene in the old town, staying there painting while it's still daylight. At the end of the day on Sunday, all the paintings are collected and judged by the Montmorillonais Artisan Community.

My easel was set up on the Vieux de Pont, looking down over the Gartempe. Your Aunt walked over the bridge and stood behind me. I could feel her energy from the very first time. Bella came past many times that weekend. When everybody gathered at the end of the festival to view the finished paintings in the Cité de L'Ecrit Gallerie, she whispered to me, "Yours is the best no matter what they say."

Enthralled by her beautiful story of their meeting, I don't want to interrupt, but have to ask, "Did you win the competition?"

"Non, of course not. The same painter from the old family who are patrons of the Montmorillonais Arts won the prize. Somebody from their family wins every year." she says, as if she expects I would know the story.

"All the paintings are then for sale and mine was the first to sell. Sold, to the red headed English girl with the beautiful smile, Bella who became my love. Bella never went back to England, she finished her story of the festival, sending it back by post to her editor. Included with that article was her resignation."

I have so many questions buzzing around in my head, but

Sophie seems relaxed and keeps talking.

"She studied French at school, loving French history, her favourite time, the 100 Years War in the 1400s between the English and the French.

"Eleanor of Aquitaine was her infatuation. We survived on Bella's royalties, her articles written for English travel magazines were very popular. If I sold a painting it was a bonus, we would take a little trip. Wanting a simple life, growing our own vegetables, loving our art, literature and each other."

Sophie looks up at me with moist eyes.

Now I understand why she has tried to avoid me. All her memories of their time together, here in this ramshackle space, and that enchanted garden. Leaving here would be like losing Bella all over again.

She draws herself up and suddenly appears cross with me again.

"Why have you come?" not giving me a moment to reply she gains pace, "Of course, it's the house, isn't it?" The Notaire said maybe one day somebody would come, but I thought he was wrong. After five years, I thought we were safe." She looks at the blue and white urn on the sideboard beside the sofa, and over at Biscuit.

This is all getting too freaky for me, I stand up, shaking my head as I look at what I thought was a pretty vase.

"Is this my aunt Bella?" Not sure what is appropriate I put my hand gently on the urn. "I should go, Madame Le Foy, I work at La Terrace in the afternoons." Thinking I need fresh air and some time to think over the last few hours, but I just can't leave letting her think I am just here to turf her out of her home. "You're wrong, I didn't know about the house, I have no intention of taking it from you." Not meaning to sound aggressive my voice comes out louder than I intend. "This is a shock for both of us and I ... I," taking a deep breath to calm my stuttering, "I really just want to be friends, if it's not too painful for you, and find out a little more about Bella."

Having waited so many weeks to say these words I can't stop them tumbling out.

"I was a lot like my father and nothing like my mother, but now they are gone. I feel as though Bella wanted me to come here and find you, maybe I can help in some way?" Not really sure what help I can be to anybody but thinking it's the right thing to say. My moving towards the door unsettles Biscuit, and he rubs up against my legs.

"Looks like you have a friend," Sophie says more gently.

"Maybe tomorrow we can take a walk around the town and talk more of Bella?"

"Yes, I would really like that," I say, thankful that things have ended on a happier note than they started, rushing to let myself out before her mood changes, Sophie calls after me.

"See you on the bridge *à dix heures*," she lapses into French.

"Yes, see you at ten Madame Le Foy," I reply.

"Oh, you can call me Sophie," her response drifts on the breeze.

Chapter 17

Days since Christmas have gone quickly but not fast enough for me.

Everything closes for two weeks, I am desperately trying to get my plans off the ground for the shop. Notaires, bank managers, *mairie* Town Planning, anybody else that I could possibly need to get answers from for my project are still on Christmas *vacances*.

Buying property in France you must first have a French bank account. So, after my appointment with the Credit Mutuel manager, at the Montmorillon branch, (involving swag loads of paperwork), I have a French bank account. Transferring 60,000 euros of my cash into the French account will be plenty to cover the purchase of the shop, agent's fees and repairs, including paying the outstanding Notaire fees on Rue Puits Cornet.

Hero tells me to be patient, it's the first rule of thumb when you do anything in France. Imagine how long it will take and triple it. My application to the *mairie* to obtain a permit for an esoteric bookshop with permission to serve wine has been submitted. As long as I don't want to serve hard liquor such as whiskey or brandy, hopefully I can obtain a licence for my business. The little shop is owned by the Montmorillon *mairie*, but as they are keen to encourage new business, Hero thinks they will sell the building to me. With the proviso it must remain a shop. Giving this undertaking, that I intend to keep it as a business downstairs, I will be able to live above on the top two floors.

My deadline is mid-May for staying in Kim's gîte, only four months away. That will give her time to get the terrace ready for the summer.

There is already water and electricity running in the old

shop, but I will have to do a few minor repairs before I can live upstairs. Damp patches in the attic indicate the roof will need repairing. Moving out the resident pigeons will be the next job. My attic has provided a warm winter home for them.

Jane has offered her husband Mark's assistance with the broken windows. Hero's lovely mum Pat, is a painter and decorator, very happy to help me with advise on how and where to buy the paint for the walls. Trading her expertise for a lifetime of tarot readings.

Reluctance to tell my new friends about my esoteric lifestyle has been completely unfounded. Before I have even signed on the dotted line my client list is steadily growing. Everybody is very supportive and enthusiastic. Having another interesting business in Montmorillon just brings in more tourism, which eventually means more people in cafes and craft shops.

Not everybody will be interested in a tarot reading, they will be welcome to browse through the books and enjoy a glass of wine or a cup of coffee. Brigitte is happy to translate my readings for her French friends until I get passed my "Franglais," the word used by most of the French community, to describe our mixture of English and French.

Kim has a huge cellar full of old furniture, she says I am welcome to drag it across the laneway. We will have to enlist the help of some young French strong lads to hoist it up the stairs. It seems every eventuality has been covered if we could just get the paperwork done.

Even Sophie has softened, offering me boxes of Bella's history and art books to sort through. Spending many walks together, becoming more comfortable in each others' company. Now that she knows my plans to live above my own shop, her concerns seem to have eased over Rue Puits

Cornet.

Planning to arrange everything with the Notaire, the house is to be gifted to Sophie, putting the titles into her name as a surprise. Imagining the look on her face when I say the house is hers, makes my heart want to burst. It just seems the right thing to do, I feel in my spirit this is why Bella's angel has summoned me here.

Like many French country houses, Bella's *maison* comes with a separate garden plot, five hundred metres past the house, along Rue Puits Cornet lane on the river side, is a walled garden. The Notaire mentioned two titles, but not the extra garden.

Sophie brought me to see it on our last walk. The old wooden door sitting firmly in a stone surround looks like an ancient door from a castle cellar. Stepping through the gateway revealed a magical secret space leading down to the river through a plantation of bamboo. Completely screened from the river and the road. Weeping willows sweep the riverbank and provide a private oasis, stone pathways criss-cross down through the bamboo forest opening to a sunny patch peeping through to the river. A rusty old iron table and chairs are propped against an open stone shed with running water, and a chimenea for a fire on a chilly day.

"Oh, Sophie what a perfect hideaway," imagining being a child looking for fairies and goblins. If ever they could exist they would be in this garden.

"We fell in love with the bamboo forests of Japan, so tranquil and calming. Bella believed in the life-giving energy that plants bring, so we planted our own Bamboo forest."

Delighted with this beautiful memory, I am touched that Sophie has chosen to share this with me.

Now I understand why the Notaire mentioned two titles for Bella's house, one for no 32 and one for the secret garden.

"On hot summer days we would come here and swim in the river and lay under the cool of the bamboo canopy."

It's hard to imagine hot summer days but I know they will come soon enough. Another season of different festivals and outdoor music concerts, everybody talks about the joyful summer in Montmorillon.

Bella lived for love and nature, I feel so connected to her.

The days are getting lighter and longer, we have the fête d'hiver at the *Vieux Palais* this coming weekend to celebrate the end of Winter.

Inviting Sophie to come along and meet my friends was a big step for me. She says she has always been too shy to mix with many of the newcomers, worried she struggles with her English. I have told her how friendly everybody is and she seems to be looking forward to the festival.

Held on the banks of the Gartempe in the grounds of the old Palais de Justice, in the early evening there will be food, French music of Edith Piaf, flame throwing, gypsy guitarists, dancing and open fires to keep us warm on the outside, hot chocolate and mulled wine to warm us up on the inside.

Each day, more and more, little things make me feel sure that my decision to start my life over in Montmorillon is the right one. The sense of community here is heart-warming. Eventually having my own nest to invite friends to, I will be able to repay all the kindness that has been shown to me.

Palais de Justice, Montmorillon

Chapter 18

Mother Nature has decided that spring should come early. It's still a few weeks 'till March, but the birds are singing spring song and all the creepers are budding. Bulbs frozen in the winter ground have pushed their green stems through the hard soil and the air is starting to smell sweet from the first cherry blossoms. Biscuit is running ahead of me, just so happy to feel the sunshine on his golden coat. Now Sophie has started to paint again, she has agreed to let me help with walking the dog. This is a real stepping stone in our friendship.

Biscuit was her last present to Bella, just months before she passed away. Sophie's portrayal of that morning was heart-breaking. Walking in, singing happy birthday to Bella, with puppy Biscuit in her arms. In the hope that the little bundle of joy "Biscuit" would entice Bella out into the garden again, to feel the sunshine on her face, and the warm snuggle of his little body lying beside her, snoozing in the sun. Bella passed away just weeks later, sleeping on the daybed, sun filtering through the silver birch, over her curls, on to biscuits head in her lap. Sophie went into the house to bring her a cup of tea and when she came out Bella had slipped away.

Bella wanted to be cremated, her ashes sprinkled in their secret garden, but Sophie has not been able to let go of her. Even Bella's clothes still sit in a trunk beside their bed.

On days like this I can feel Bella's spirit around me and so wish I could speak with her. She has come to me in my dreams several times, not speaking, just drifting peacefully.

The Gartempe River is running fast beside us, swollen with the winter rains and in a hurry to make its way through the Vienne. Biscuit runs ahead, barking at the turkey ducks. He responds well to me now, so I let him have more freedom on our walks. It's nearly lunchtime so the park is deserted, everybody at home or packed into the little French cafes for

127

the compulsory midday to 2pm three-course lunch. Something I still can't get used to, Midday is just too early for lunch. Sophie has soup on the cooker, we will have a bowl together when I drop Biscuit back home.

He is so far ahead, I can only just make out the flash of his coat, disappearing around the bend. As I get closer to the car park, I notice a small white van. Probably just somebody parked to enjoy the river, eating their lunch. Biscuit is nowhere to be seen. Looking past the car, getting anxious to get Biscuit back on the lead, I start calling out to him, whistling loud, calling his name, there is still no sign of him.

Something just doesn't feel right, the butterflies in my stomach are making me feel nervous. Reaching the car, intending to just nod and acknowledge the driver, I am stopped in my tracks. The front passenger door springs open banging my leg, knocking me off balance, falling backwards putting my hand out to break the fall, I feel a sharp jab through my wrist. Dirty puddle water splashes up all over my clothes. With my heart racing with fear, an empty whiskey bottle rolls onto the ground beside the door. I look up into the boozy face of Jean-Claude.

"Shit, you idiot, what are you doing?" Screaming at him with all the strength I can muster, my wrist is killing me. I try to regain my balance and get out of the puddle, it's hard to push myself up with one hand. Lifting his foot he kicks my shoulder backwards, my heart is pounding, screaming at top of my voice for Biscuit. Not sure of what Jean-Claude is intending to do, just hoping the threat of the dog will scare him away.

Thank the angels he has been drinking, he is not that steady on his feet, as I draw myself up to face him he spits in my face.

"So, Miss Aussie Izzy, you think you're too good for me?"

His disgusting breath makes me feel like I am going to puke, he grabs my arm and puts his face into mine. Using my last bit of energy, I scream so loud, pushing him backwards. Making a crunching sound he bangs his head on the bonnet of the car, giving me a second to look around. Biscuit appears wet and soggy from the river, running between us baring his teeth.

Jean-Claude bangs the door shut, reversing. Narrowly missing the picnic table behind him. Watching him zig-zag down the road, counting myself lucky for Biscuit's better late than never appearance, I feel suddenly sick and vomit, just missing poor Biscuit. He is nudging me, whining, aware that something is not right.

My wrist is swelling, and my bottom is sore from falling in the puddle. With clothes covered in mud and Biscuit safely clipped on the lead, we start the slow limp back down the lane to find Sophie.

Hot tears are dripping down my face by the time I push open the gates to the garden, well and truly in shock at how close I have come to being more seriously attacked. Biscuit runs ahead to the glasshouse where Sophie is painting. Taking one look at Biscuit, who looks like a water-logged river monster, she runs past him.

"Oh, *mon dieu*, what's happened?"

She looks me up and down and hugs me to her, I wince holding my arm and sobbing into her shoulder.

"That bastard Jean-Claude," is all I can blurt out through the sobs.

Sophie seats me carefully on the sofa, moving my wrist gently with her fingers.

"You are very lucky, I think that it is not broken."

She bathes my gravel rash hands and makes me a cup of coffee, beside which she sits a glass of brandy. Looking into my face, she is so full of concern.

While I recount what happened, the brandy starts to warm me, slowly calming my nerves, easing the dull ache in my wrist. Biscuit is sitting with his head across my feet, his big sad eyes showing his concern.

As I unwind, Sophie winds up, gathering speed like a storm, she spits out the words like a venomous snake.

"Il est de la merde, il devrait être jeté en prison, c'est une mauvaise famille."

Now I feel like I should calm Sophie, she is saying he should go to prison the little shit. Something about him coming from a bad family.

"Sophie, he is a drunk, he needs help. His ego took a battering, he has asked me out a few times, but I want nothing to do with him."

"Of course you don't," she softens her tone.

"He needs a doctor and rehabilitation, not prison, perhaps the police could talk to his grandparents."

I surprise myself with my own reasoning.

Exhausted and in no mood to see police or argue with Sophie, I ask her to walk me home to the gîte. Strangely my anger towards John Claude has turned to pity. Sophie seems more concerned about the whole episode than me. Perhaps she knows more about Jean-Claude Allardet than she is letting on.

Turning the key, pushing in the gîte door I feel shaky again and ask Sophie if she will stay with me for a little while.

This is the first time that Sophie has actually come into my space, I can see her hesitate at the door but then she follows me inside.

My calmness seems to add to Sophie's concern,

"I think you are in shock, I don't know if you should be on your own tonight."

"I will be fine Sophie, maybe tomorrow we should tell the police, perhaps they can talk with his family. He is just a bully, he had been drinking, I really don't think it was premeditated." Not wanting to think of the possibility he has been watching me take Biscuit down to the park, and was waiting for me.

It seems strange to be sitting here with Sophie, we are usually either walking the dog, or having coffee in her kitchen.

My nerves have calmed but I really don't want to be left on my own just yet, trying to think of an excuse to keep Sophie here, but not appear like a sook, I spy my cards.

"Perhaps you can help me to read the cards?" Not waiting for an answer, I reach over with my good hand, putting the silky bundle between us on the sofa, ready to share this part of myself with Sophie.

Understanding how difficult this might be for her, this is probably the first time she has touched the cards since Bella died. She watches me intently,

"You have the gift like Bella, you were right to come Izzy, I think Bella has guided you here."

Shuffling the cards is difficult, my right hand is all puffy, the bruising just starting to come out and I can feel a throbbing through my wrist. Using my left hand I swish the cards around, laying the cards in a pyramid, I still my mind and speak to my angels.

"Am I on my karmic path? Help me, is this where I should be?"

I realise how much I have grown emotionally by my reactions to today's events. Feeling strong enough to see Jean-Claude as somebody who needs help, not a real threat to me. Not feeling the need to run back into my shell for cover.

Choosing three cards I build my pyramid and lay a final card in the centre. Sophie is quiet as a mouse as I turn the cards over one by one.

"The Fool," on his merry way his little dog by his side, off on an adventure, not a care in the world, look ahead not behind, don't let trivial details get in your way. I love The Fool for his beautiful childish innocence.

"The Tower," struck by lightning. This card sends a warning of unexpected events, everything changing, the castle dwellers leaping out the window as the tower catches fire. It can be a warning of completely unexpected happenings. Not wanting to dwell on The Tower I carry on to my third card.

"Six of Pentacles," a turn for the better, your turn to receive, favour and prosperity. One of the most positive pentacles in the pack. So far my life has followed a pattern of necessity, maybe it's finally my time to receive good karma and realise my dreams.

Looking into Sophie's face, trying to judge her response. I am sure she must have done many readings with Bella.

Bella's tarot packs still sit on the big sideboard at the house.

"Go on then," she urges me to turn over the final card, the driver of my pyramid.

"The Magician," I let out a happy sigh, Sophie smiles. The Magician says I will have success with new ventures. Good communication, turning ideas into reality. A triumph and creative success. There is risk and opportunity. The Magician has the skills to succeed, clarity of my mind, creativity, a passionate heart and practicability.

Assuring Sophie I will be fine and just needing a good night's sleep, I wish her; "A bientôt."

"A demain," she says softly and heads out into a moonlit night.

Tossing and turning, pain in my wrist stops me from having a good night's sleep. Replaying over and over what happened at the park.

Convincing myself, Jean-Claude is just a sad case and not really a threat to me. My reading, ending with The Magician was exciting, but The Tower sends chills up my spine. Eventually I drift off, dreaming of Bella sitting on the swing, her red hair blowing in the breeze.

Tarot pyramid,

The Fool, The Tower, Six of Pentacles, The Magician

Rider-Waite Tarot Deck

Chapter 19

Completion day for the shop has finally arrived. Hero has prepared me for at least two hours of bottom numbing boredom in the Notaire's office. At least our appointment is this morning, so I will finally have the keys and can spend all afternoon measuring up and making plans.

Every page of the contract will have to be initialed and the final payment made by cheque. The keys will then be handed to me. The *Notaire* represents the *mairee* so they will not be present. I will own the property but have to wait for permission to open my business. This must still be passed by the Montmorillon Commerce Committee.

Paying by cheque seems so archaic to me, we haven't used cheques in Australia for years. Cheques in France are still good as gold, and you can go to prison for writing a dud one.

Thank goodness I have had Maisons Rurales to sort out all the translations and explain the complicated process. Getting a permit for the shop will just be par for the course. The *mairie* have said I may have to meet with the committee before they decide. Hero does not seem to think it will be any problem. The town is keen to encourage new enterprise.

As the Notaire signs on the dotted line, Hero witnesses our signatures, I can feel my heart wants to explode. This is the start of a long-held dream, I just wish Dad was here with me.

Monsieur Duval hands me the heavy set of keys, I can't stop smiling. We walk out of his office into the bright sunshine. Hero yells out, "Well done, Izzy, see you tonight." Jumping into her car, rushing for her next appointment, completion has gone over time by half an hour and she hates to keep her clients waiting.

Wishing I could see my friends and celebrate sooner than this evening, I walk back, only down the hill, and over the new bridge. Relishing the time to let this morning sink in. I have done this walk so many times, today it feels so different. Being a home and business owner will really make me a part of the community. Feeling the weight of the keys jingling in my pocket, humming a little tune, I stroll back into Montmorillon, this special little town that is now my new home.

Sophie has even agreed to come along and join us tonight. Her confidence with my friends has grown, we all try to speak as much French as we can. Even Sophie had to agree how much fun we all had together at the le fête d'hiver.

Her self-imposed isolation since Bella's death seems to be giving way, slowly coming out of her shell. In a way, we are both changing ourselves, learning to share our newfound friendship. My self-confidence is growing, for the first time I can remember, I actually like myself, finally accepting that people enjoy my company.

If only Hero didn't have another appointment. I really want to share my joy with somebody. Kim doesn't open till 3pm and I don't like to invade her private time. I have booked us all in for dinner at Crêperie du Brouard, it's my favourite fun place to eat. Franc the host and his wife do the yummiest galettes and delicious crêpes suzettes. Tonight, I am treating everybody to celebrate getting the keys to No 1 Rue Vieux Pont. I am going to wear one of my charity shop outfits and even allow myself a dessert. It's still chilly at night but come summer, Franc will put chairs, tables and bright umbrellas overlooking the river. It's going to be a perfect summer. My Wheel of Fortune has lifted me up and even my nasty scare with Jean-Claude won't dampen my enthusiasm.

Sophie finds it hard to believe how much of a loner I was at home. Her personality is warm and she is very funny, although she doesn't see it in herself. After months of me wondering her age she let slip that Bella was older than her. She seems so much wiser than me and has done so much in her life, when actually there is probably only a few years between us. I feel like a child when I spend time with her, maybe her sadness at losing Bella has taken her childish enthusiasm.

Walking past the Creperie I continue up the steep hill past La Caverne Bar, deciding to pop in and see my friend James who runs "The Glass Key" the English bookshop in the Cité de L'Ecrit. He has been so encouraging about my idea to open an esoteric boutique.

Sophie was introduced to James through Bella, he is one of the only English residents here that she has stayed in contact with since Bella died.

James reminds me of a merry wizard from a children's novel, white hair and beard, always a smile and a story to tell. Having run his bookshop for eight years, he has loads of good tips to pass on to me, speaking wonderful French. I hope I can mirror his communication skills with my French customers. I can't wait to show him the keys to my dream.

Pushing open the door, James peers up at me over a pile of books on his corner desk. "Ah, Izzy, what a lovely surprise."

"Bonjour, James, how you doing?" replying and smiling ear to ear.

Not waiting for him to reply I pull out the keys and dangle them in front of him.

"I settled on the shop this morning." Beaming at him.

"Well, welcome to Montmorillon Commerce. You know you only have to ask, Izzy, I will do anything to help a fellow Montmorillon Merchant. We need more like you to get this town back on its feet."

I can feel myself glowing in James' praise, it's so wonderful to feel wanted in this community.

"What are you doing to celebrate?" James asks me. I feel a touch of the guilts as tonight is just for the girls.

"Sorry, James, we're going to the Crêperie for dinner, but it's just the girls." I make a pretend sad face.

"Ah then, just as well I have a little surprise." He reaches behind him and pulls out a box of Bordeaux red wine. "We can't let this day pass without a little toast." I am touched by his thoughtfulness, and we drink to good luck and good friends. "Bonne Chance, mon amie."

Promising to take him up on his offer of help, I leave and walk back down the steep cobblestone lane.

I can't wait a minute longer, running over the old bridge, smiling up at the old black cat sign dangling above the door at No 1. There are so many keys, but I remember watching Hero when she showed me the building all those weeks ago.

The largest key opens the shutter door and looks like a relic from a castle. Creaking, the shutter gives way, revealing the studded solid front door. Third time lucky I find the right key, and with a bit of jiggling the key finally turns.

Propping the door open with an old box to let in a ray of light, there is no electricity connected but the wiring is there. The connection was arranged for last week but this is rural France, if the appointment falls near the end of the day or lunch break time you just go to the end of the queue.

Daylight gives me enough illumination to make my way to the two windows on one side of the room. Forcing open the catch and sliding the iron rod along the shutters I fling them open. The light floods into the room and the view out over the river is perfect. Turkey ducks are flapping about below, and I can't wait to see how beautiful this room will be with a big clean out. The back of the room has two small steps leading up to another smaller room, which will be a perfect space for my readings. The window in the back of this room looks down the Gartempe, my imagination is already running wild with visions of tapestries and rich velvets and heavy candlesticks to change this to a welcoming cave.

Deciding it's too dangerous to go upstairs till I have proper lighting, I decide to sit for a moment in the middle of the front room. I have waited for this moment a lifetime and take time to thank my angels and Bella for bringing me here. "Oh, Dad, you would be so proud of me," whispering to him, "I promise I will make this a success."

It takes me ages to lock up again and I really don't want to leave. Tonight will be so much fun and tomorrow my next chapter begins.

The Glass Key, English bookshop, Cité de L'Ecrit, Montmorillon

Chapter 20

Our girls' night at the Creperie was a huge success and the perfect celebration to commemorate the start of my little shop "Le Petit Chat Noir". I have always believed that black cats bring luck and it's a lucky omen for me. The medieval archangel above the door will watch over me, making me feel certain about my future here.

The *mairie* has been in touch and arranged a meeting with the Commerce Committee. Seems there are a few issues to be cleared up before they will grant my licence to open the *magasin*. Hero knows the most about all this sort of thing so she is coming to the meeting with me.

Most of the committee members work in stores of their own so the meeting has been arranged for 7pm, that will give Hero time to lock up the office and walk over with me to the *mairie* building behind the tourist information on the square.

Not her usual bubbly self, Hero walks in silence along the place du Maréchal LeClerc, past the Palais café full of French friends meeting for apéros after work. Looking in through the bright windows as we pass we both say in unison, "Wish we were going in there."

"Izzy, I had a few phone calls today from James."

"Oh really?" I reply.

"It seems that a few of the Cité de L'Ecrit owners are still away on *vacances*. There might not be enough people at the meeting to make a decision."

Now I understand Hero's glum mood, she was trying to find a way to tell me that things may not be as easy as we expected tonight. I assumed it was just a *fait accompli*, that everybody would be happy about another shop to entice more tourists to Montmorillon.

As we step inside the glass doors to the *mairie*, I see there is a small group of people standing in the foyer. Their hushed

French conversation makes me feel nervous. Hero links her arm through mine for reassurance. We sit on the chairs outside the meeting room and James comes over to join us.

We are all shown into the meeting room which looks more like an antique library, finding our position around the table.

Monsieur Pierine introduces himself to everybody for my benefit, I am sure everybody else knows who he is, the chairman of the Commerce Committee. Things start off orderly in slow French so I am able to understand parts of it, Hero is trying hard to translate the bits in between for me.

Monsieur Pierine asks me to outline my plan for the shop. Speaking slowly I wait for Hero to translate my responses. He looks again at his notes.

The chairman addresses me in French and Hero translates. I keep my eyes in contact with Monsieur Pierine, wanting him to see that I am serious and capable of my new plan.

I explain that it is not good to have a shop empty that sits overlooking the old bridge, and will entice more commerce for Montmorillon. I don't want to work against the other bookstore owners but with them. Perhaps I can advertise things for the other booksellers in my window, and that will draw people over the bridge, into the old medieval town? Hero translates my responses and the other committee members nod their heads in approval.

"And the issue of selling wine, Madame Baker?"

I take a deep breath and reply, "I won't be selling wine Monsieur, it will be *gratuit*, for my customers while they browse in my shop."

"Café?" he replies. Thinking quickly, I decide to stand my ground.

"I would like to make a small charge for coffee or tea," I reply nervously.

Hero looks at me, squeezing my hand under the table, giving me a much needed boost.

Monsieur Pierine scribbles down some notes, closes his

folder and rises.

Thanking everybody for their attendance, he turns and leaves the room.

Leaning over I whisper in James' ear, "What happens now?"

James replies, "You'll probably wait weeks for an answer and then fingers crossed, a yes. Your biggest problem will be getting all the paperwork processed in time for the book fair, Salon Du Livre.

"Come on, Izzy, let's go for a drink, you gave it your best shot, that's all you can do." Hero leads the way out onto the now dark street.

"Joining us, James?" Hero tilts her head in the direction of *Le Palais Bar*.

"Why not, in for a penny in for a pound," he smiles trying to lighten my mood.

Hero tries to cheer me up as we sip our beers. "I've been to many of those types of meetings over the years. I think that Monsieur Pierine might just surprise you. He's very supportive of new ventures and keen to see Montmorillon prosper. He didn't say an outright NO, so you never know."

We all chime in, "It will be alright in the end and if it's not alright it's not the end." Laughing together.

Not expecting this hurdle to jump over, I know I have little choice but to leave it up to Fortune's Wheel. At the very least I have a place to call home, with a little *bonne chance* I will have "Le Petit Chat Noir."

The Crêperie

Chapter 21

Over the next few weeks I decide to focus all my efforts on upstairs at No 1. Worrying is not going to change the outcome of my application to the *mairie* for the licence, making Le Petit Chat Noir a reality. May is quickly approaching and I need a place to lay my head.

Now the electricity and water are finally connected. Upstairs two floors have been scrubbed clean, de-cobwebbed, and with the assistance of the kind *mairie* maintenance man, Monsieur Beauvois, we have re-housed the pigeons that had made my attic their home.

Sophie has been a star, driving me about in her little red Citroen, picking up everything from toilet seats to a new vacuum cleaner. She is so focussed and won't even let me look at fluffy things like curtains till all the practical things are done. At the end of our long days cleaning we hardly muster the energy to walk back over to her place for dinner.

Sophie paints in the mornings and gets the dinner prepared before joining me at the shop. Over dinner we plan the next day's work, then Sophie and Biscuit walk me back to the gîte in the moonlight.

The days are getting longer and the air is heavy with the scent of roses and honeysuckle. With most of the hard work done I can start to think about my favourite part, the finishing touches. After pulling off an old temporary wall, in what will be my kitchen, we found pretty blue and white tiles. Years of paint scraped back they now have a new lease of life. Old cupboards from Kim's cellar are now duck egg blue, rubbing them back just a touch has given my little home a touch of French shabby chic. Under the layers of vinyl on the floor were lovely big dark floorboards. Claude from Panier Sympa, has loaned me his sander. After a few quick lessons and much hilarity, Sophie and I have transformed my floors. The sander was so powerful it knocked us both off our feet.

Mr. Bricolage, the local handyman store, had rolls of pale blue and white wallpaper at 2 euros a roll. Just perfect for the living room, which will double as my bedroom. Offers of second hand furniture have been kindly accepted, a large sofa bed is waiting for me in Kim's front salon.

La Petite Mercerie, being just two doors down the lane from me is such a temptation, a treasure trove of fabrics and ribbons. Popping in to say hi to Jane, I always leave with my arms full of pretty things. At the back of the fabric room, we found a roll of gold and sky-blue tapestry, which I will use for the curtains. Having failed needlecraft in High School, I have begged help from Jane the master of the sewing machine. Loads of Sophie's old cushions will be covered in a pattern of tiny blue tits, robins and butterflies, three of my favourite things.

After weeks of hard work, but loving every minute of it, I finally have the perfect little home upstairs. While Sophie and I have scrubbed and cleaned, Pat has worked on my shutters and taken little black cat away to be given a shiny new coat of paint. Hopefully everything can be hinged and screwed back into place on the facade soon.

This morning, Sophie knocked at the gîte door, an hour earlier than expected. Still in my early morning haze and wearing my jammies, I got a surprise to see her on the terrace in the early sun.

Letting her in I stifled a yawn.

"Bonjour, Isabella." My curiosity is immediately alerted. Sophie looks like the cat that swallowed the cream. "Nous allons a Poitier."

"Que?" I reply, still trying to wake myself up.

Sophie chatters on in half French, half English, telling me we both work so hard but today we take a rest. We are driving to Poitiers the beautiful medieval city just an hour from Montmorillon.

We can take a walk by the river, maybe do a little shopping, and visit some of the places she has told me about. My sightseeing so far has been limited to Montmorillon and a couple of little villages that Hero and Pat have driven me to see, so I am very excited to visit Poitiers as I know it was built by the Romans and featured in the 100 year war. Eleanor of Aquitaine resided at times in Poitiers and in 1152 married the future King Henry 11 of England in Poitiers Cathedral. The royal parliament moved from Paris to Poitiers. The Palais de Justice still has references to Eleanor of Aquitaine, and in 1429 was the site of Joan of Arc's wrongful trial. With all of this whirring through my mind Sophie senses my excitement. Smiling at me she knows she has won me over.

Still feeling that Sophie is up to something I run upstairs for a quick shower. "It's going to be a beautiful sunny spring day," Sophie shouts up the stairs, "can't be all work and no playing."

Feeling guilty that I should be working, but relishing the chance to have a day surrounded by history in Poitier. I pull on my new jeans, surprising myself by doing up the zipper easily. My walks have been substituted for renovations, it appears that running up and down stairs carrying painting materials and lugging furniture have had a positive effect on my body. Encouraged by Kim I have left my hair to its own flow, now long enough to pull back into a ponytail. Sophie is getting impatient and calls up the stairs "On y va, on y va, let's get going."

Driving out over the new bridge and around the ring road we take the turn-off to Chauvigny, Biscuit sitting behind us has his head resting in between us, he seems as excited as me about a day out.

As we drive along Sophie tells me that her family come

from a small hamlet 20 kilometres north of Poitiers, so she knows the town well. Her uncle was killed before she was born, he worked at the Poitiers Railway Station which was heavily bombed in 1944. Thinking to myself of all the connections between us, Harriet pops into my mind and a vision of her leading her neighbours to the bomb shelters in London.

We drive in silence for a few miles each in thought of how horribly cruel war can be. As we round the bend Sophie pulls into a panorama parking spot. There before us sits the majestic ruins of the Chauvigny Chateau. Biscuit jumps out happy to be in the fresh air and Sophie climbs up onto the stone wall in front of the car. Holding out her hand for me she pulls me up beside her, pointing out the old drawbridge and two remaining towers.

"They have birds of prey in the castle and every day at 3pm you can sit and watch them being fed, maybe another time we do that?" Sophie is clearly enjoying being my tour guide.

Jumping back in the car we take the road through Chauvigny past the market square and over the river, heading out up the hill, soon there are fields of gold and lavender as far as we can see.

There are no stone walls here, just rows of sunflowers that meet the tiny road that cuts a path, occasionally we drive through little woods with sun sending down beams through the dense foliage.

Sophie says in the last months of the war, many soldiers parachuted into these woods. It's not hard to imagine the scenes that I have watched in many war movies. Old derelict barns that would make perfect hideaways for resistance fighters taking cover from the Nazis. We are just ten minutes away from the Vienne River, which marked the border between occupied and unoccupied France.

Soon the rolling fields give way to hamlets followed by more and more factories, this must be the outskirts of

Poitiers. Just as I think how industrial this has become we take a left onto a ring road that brings us into the city. Either side of us are huge stone walls with imposing French houses clinging to their sides. Following along the river, which winds its way through the city, Sophie points out St Pierre Cathedral in the distance and the rooftop of Notre Dame Romanesque church.

The roads are more like laneways built for horse and carriage, not 21st century traffic. Sophie navigates the one-way system skilfully and I am so glad she is not relying on me to get us from A to B. I am already completely lost, we seem to come into the city from the opposite direction. Beside the road runs an impressive wrought-iron fence, we pull up outside huge gates and a sign that reads Blossac Parc.

"Let's go for a walk and enjoy the sunshine." Sophie grabs Biscuit's lead and a picnic basket.

"God I'm starving," realising I haven't even had breakfast, last night's dinner was just an avocado baguette.

Blossac Parc is a green oasis right in the centre of Poitiers. So not what I had expected. We meander along the stone pathways and Biscuit pulls eagerly at the lead anxious to explore all the new smells. Sophie points to a little pond and we make our way to a sunny clearing, spreading the blanket, lifting treats from the basket. Cognac pate, cherry tomatoes, mushroom quiche, cheese and baguettes, not forgetting generous slices of tarte tatin. Feeling more like a sleep than exploring old buildings, I rest my head onto Biscuit who is already snoozing in the sun. This is such a treat after all our hard work on the shop.

"Come on sleepy heads." Sophie packs up our picnic and Biscuit stands ready for his next adventure.

We decide to leave the car and walk up Rue de Carnot, which brings us right onto Poitiers Square. The 18th century Hotel de Ville sits proudly with a commanding view over the town. Small cobblestone walkways lead off the square down to the Romanesque Notre Dame and past the Palais de Justice. Still used today, the magnificent Palace is the home of the old law courts. Dating back to the Dukes of Aquitaine in the tenth century.

Sophie waits outside with Biscuit while I wander through the great halls. Imagining Eleanor of Aquitaine who became Queen of England, here in her famed Court of Love. Eleanor's court focused on symbolic ritual and courtly love, attracting artists and poets who contributed to the growth of culture and arts in Poitiers.

Not wanting to drag myself away, but conscious that Sophie is waiting on the streets outside, I step out into the sunshine.

Linking my arm through Sophie's we stroll back to the Citroen.

"Can we take a trip one day to Fontevraud Abbey in Chinon?" I ask Sophie, not wanting to push her generosity of spirit.

"Yes of course," she smiles at me, "it was one of Bella's favourite days out."

It is the place where Eleanor of Aquitaine was laid to rest in 1204.

"For now, we had better get back to work."

It's nearly dusk as we drive back into Montmorillon and I wonder why Sophie parks on the square. Usually she would drive past La Terrace and over the Vieux Pont, the old bridge, parking down behind the Roman des Saveurs on the river.

"Why are we parking here, Sophie?" I ask her, intrigued.

"You will see, come on."

As we round the corner into Rue Vieux Pont I can just make out a little group of people standing in front of my shop.

Pat and her husband Keith are standing in their overalls, Kim is holding a bottle of champagne, and Jane beaming ear to ear is pointing overhead. Hero comes running across the bridge as fast as her high heels will let her.

"Phew, wait for me," she pants.

"Surprise," they all yell as Pat pulls a sheet off the façade of the building.

"Oh my," I exclaim, not believing what I can see.

All the shutters are back in place, painted pretty cornflower blue, the once rusty hinges all shiny and new, the little black cat given a new shiny black coat, and best of all, a brand new sign hanging over the doorway.

Hand-painted, exquisite black calligraphy on a pale blue background.

"Le Petit Chat Noir."

"We didn't want you to see it in stages." says Pat. "We wanted you to see it all finished."

Turning to Sophie who is looking very happy with herself for distracting me all day.

"Thank you so much everybody, time for champers"

We all step inside, Kim pops the cork,

"Here's to Izzy and Le Petit Chat Noir!"

The Magician from my reading springs to mind, and I thank Bella for guiding me here, such a wonderful community which I now feel a part of.

"Rush hour" Montmorillon

Chapter 22

Kim and I work together to get her terrace ready for the spring.

After steam cleaning all the paving, trimming wisteria and grape vines, we are ready to recover the outdoor tables. Am on my back, with the staple gun finishing off the edges, while Kim assembles all the new umbrellas. Pat's newly-finished "La Terrasse Salon de Thé," sign is hoisted up and screwed into place.

I love the way this little neighbourhood comes together to get the work done. While I still wait for my permits, it's great to be able to repay the friendship and hard work that everyone has put into Le Petit Chat Noir.

Kim rewards us all with a cream tea, plates of warm scones just from the oven, lashings of whipped cream and homemade cassis. Mouths too full for talking we are all tucking into this delicious spread.

While we enjoy our afternoon tea Kim tells us of her idea for a spring party at La Terrasse.

"What's a spring party?" Keith pipes up.

"Celebrate new growth, the start of new things," says Kim. "I thought we could wear wigs, just a fun way to get everybody together to celebrate the start of Spring."

Parties are not really my thing, I never know what to wear, and usually feel really out of it, but Kim's enthusiasm is happy to see and I nod in agreement.

Pat sees the look of concern on my face and puts her arm around my shoulder. "Don't worry, Izzy, you'll get used to Kim's parties." It's perfect timing to celebrate your new shop."

"My cellar is full of stuff, love," Kim calls back to me as she carries all our plates back inside. "You've lost so much weight there'll be lots of things to fit you."

Being so happy and absorbed in my project I feel healthier

than I ever have. Usually only wearing jeans, and baggy jumpers to cover my bulk, maybe wearing a dress might be fun for a change.

"Well if I don't get my shop permit soon there won't be a new shop," I moan.

Le Salon du Livre is in four weeks' time, a book fair that goes all weekend. It will be the perfect time for my opening. If M. Pierane could just get a move on with my permit.

Thanking Kim for the yummy refreshments, and admiring our team effort, I decide to see if Hero has heard anything from the *mairie*. They will contact her because she acted as my translator.

Walking across the square towards Maisons Rurales, Hero's office, I see her blond curls coming from outside the *mairie*. She spots me

"Izzy, Izzy, you got it!" Waving a white envelope in her hand, she hurries across the Place Du Maréchal LeClerc.

"Monsieur Pierane called me this morning and said they had made a decision. He asked me to come to his office and voila, we have it. You can open in time for the Salon du Livre, and you can offer a glass of wine, if you don't accept payment for it. They will allow you to sell coffee and tea. You're not part of the Cité de L'Ecrit, as you're on this side of the bridge, but that doesn't stop you from selling books."

I am stunned looking at this piece of paper that will allow me to start my little business.

Hero burbles on, just so happy for me. "He said the committee sees this as a positive step for the town. Hopefully this will encourage many more new-comers to set up shop in Montmorillon."

Telling Hero about Kim's idea for the party, we both agree, it's perfect timing. I will also have an official opening and invite the other bookshop owners along for a glass of champagne and extend the hand of friendship.

Hugging Hero and thanking her, I run back over the bridge

to find Sophie and tell her my brilliant news.

Chapter 23

1 Vieux Pont
86500
Montmorillon

Dear Maria

Thank you for your patience with me over my lack of correspondence. I hope that you have realised it's because everything is just falling into place for me in Montmorillon.

It's as though my aunt Bella has called me to be here. I so wish I had known her, the more I learn about her personality the more I feel we are kindred spirits.

I have so much that I want to share with you but really hoping that I can do that in person. That brings me to my next news. Finally my permit to run a business has been granted by the mairie. It came with a struggle which I will tell you more about later, the main thing for now is, I can go ahead with the shop downstairs at No 1 Vieux Pont.

With the help of my new friends here I have finished the living space upstairs. It's tiny but it's home.

There are just four weeks till the Salon du Livre, a weekend festival of books held by the Cité de L'Ecrit. My little esoteric boutique La Petit Chat Noir is beside the old bridge leading into the medieval town. Oh I can't wait for you to see it.

All the other businesses in town do special things as well to make the most of all the extra tourists here for the Salon du Livre.

I know this is a big ask but I am really hoping that you and Joe will make the trip over for my shop opening. You can stay upstairs and Sophie says I can sleep on her sofa.

Please please say you'll come. You fly into Paris then take the train to Poitiers. Sophie and I can come to pick you up from the station.

Remember your promise, Maria, you said if I settled somewhere you would come to visit?

I will send this letter by registered express post so you will have time to think about things.

It will be the summer here and so festive and warm, perfect time to leave the Melbourne winter behind.

Things have turned a corner with Sophie and we have a wonderful friendship. There are some things stirring in my heart which I don't quite understand but hope I can share with you soon. The only thing that could make me any happier would be to have you and Joe here to share my excitement.

Sending you lots of love and hugs.

Your Izzy

PS my French is coming along and I stopped biting my nails.

PPS my Wheel of Fortune sent me the Magician.

View from Sophie's house

Palais de Justice

Chapter 24

Warm spring days make Montmorillon come to life. The evenings stretch out and cafes move their seating onto the pavements. Red umbrellas pop up everywhere and Monty seems like a different town. Closed shutters now open with blankets and duvets handing over ledges to air in the warm spring breeze.

Walking along the cobbled streets I am greeted by many bonjours.

The sunshine and blue skies improve everybody's mood. One by one the members of the committee have been coming past, giving me a *bonjour* and a wave of encouragement. All curious to see what is changing about the little shop. I want to be the bridge that connects the old town to the new.

Even Jean-Claude seems to have gone to ground. I have been dreading bumping into him. Jane says she has heard from her friend at the Gendarmerie that he is living in Limoges for a while.

I miss living in Kim's little gîte, waking to the view of the Notre Dame, but my own little *maison* has a tiny glimpse down the river and Kim has kindly said I'm welcome to stretch out in the sunshine on the terrace, outside of trading hours. Sophie's magical garden is another oasis, after our hard days of renovating the shop.

Second-hand shelving from "The Glass Key," compliments of James, and from Claude's Panier Sympa, have been given a new lease of life, all placed in their new home at Le Petit Chat Noir. Hand-painted cards and crystals are due to arrive any day. Runes, wind-chimes, wizards and fairies will hang in the window. Sourced from local artists and village brocantes. Books, books and more boxes of books are waiting for me to sort through in Sophie's attic. Bella's love of historical novels is going to keep the shelves filled for months. Angel and fairy cards, mythical tarot and numerology books.

My most expensive purchase is the Delonghi coffee machine. Pretty eclectic tea and coffee mugs will brighten up the coffee corner. Kim doesn't open on Mondays or before 3pm in the winter, so I plan to make the most of those quieter times temping people in for a tarot reading and warm-up drink.

By day, I am painting, nailing and repairing. By night writing a course of notes for what I hope will be my first tarot tuition group. Starting in English and French on the days that Brigitte is available to translate.

By the end of the year I hope my French will have improved enough to fly solo.

With painted shelves still to dry properly, and everything just about ready for the opening, I decide to take Biscuit for an early walk and make the most of this beautiful spring sunshine.

Pushing open Sophie's gate I am surprised to see her sitting on the swing. She's usually already hard at work in her studio at the bottom of the garden creating another masterpiece to take to the spring brocantes. Biscuit trots up to me with his tail wagging. "Bonjour, Biscuit, my beautiful boy." He laps up my praise and rubs his head against my leg.

"I 'ave been waiting for you, Izzy, today is time for me to let go of Bella. I think we should do this together, it's what Bella would want." Without explanation, Sophie walks towards the house. Unsure what exactly she means I stay with Biscuit in the garden. Only seconds pass and Sophie walks out holding the blue and white urn to her breast.

So very unexpected, I'm not sure how to respond,

"Would you like to spread Bella's ashes today, Sophie? Set her spirit free?" I ask her gently.

"I have held onto her for too long, not wanting to let her go, but I know now that she will always be around me."

162

Putting my arm gently around Sophie's shoulder I reply softly,

"She will be around you, Sophie, I think it's a precious thing to share with you." Feeling so emotional that I will be a part of this ritual, I feel tears start to prick my eyes.

"The spring was her favourite time, everything bursting into flower, the scent on the breeze, the bird song, she loved it. Can you get Biscuit's lead? I want him to be with us, he was Bella's dog."

Together the three of us walk along Rue Puits Cornet. Sophie carrying her cherished Bella, Biscuit and I feeling the spring sun on our backs. We walk around the bend and follow the river to the picnic ground at Les Ilettes, our only company horses in the fields high above the road and the sounds of new duck families testing out the fast moving water.

Past the picnic ground, Sophie leads the way onto the pontoon jutting out over the fast-flowing Gartempe. It feels like a boat with the waters winding past taking the river on its way through the Vienne Valley.

Sophie kisses the urn and screws off the lid, lifting and tilting it up so Bella's ashes gently catch the breeze.

"Goodbye my beautiful girl, fly free." The tears run down my face as Sophie passes me the urn, I gently let the rest of Bella's ashes fall onto the breeze, and there she is taken off on the river's flow.

Standing in silence, the sun on our faces, the wheel has completed for Bella and her next journey begins.

With one hand on the lead and the other in Sophie's we stroll back in silence each with our thoughts.

Instead of walking past the secret garden to the house Sophie stops in front of the faded jade door, reaches into the pocket of her painting overalls and takes out the rusty old key. Still holding onto the urn she pushes on the door with her foot. Scraping back through months of fallen leaves the door inches open and we step into the canopy of bamboo. It's been months since Sophie first showed me the garden, the first weeks of spring sending a flourish of growth. It's like a lush green carpet.

Biscuit charges through the long growth loving this new game. We follow down through the bamboo to the ivy-covered seating at the bottom of the garden. Sophie sets the urn down on the table. Sun rays flit in and out of the bamboo and make a pattern of fairies dancing. Biscuit has had enough of playing in the long reeds and charges into the river to chase the ducks.

"Look at him, he loves to swim, just like Bella," Sophie laughs.

I give a little shiver. "It must be freezing in there."

"Can you swim?" Sophie asks me.

"Well, er yes, but at home I am scared of sharks, so I only paddle."

Sophie giggles.

"Well there are no sharks here except for Jean-Claude." Laughing, Sophie unhooks her braces and pulls her T shirt over her head. Stepping out of her overalls she yells, "Come on I'll race you, we always used to go for a swim to celebrate the start of the warmer weather."

Unashamedly, she steps out of her underwear and runs towards the water. "Come on, Izzy, no sharks today."

Sophie is into the water before I can draw breath.

I look around slightly nervous, so not used to showing my body to anybody. It's so private here, the high stone fence and bamboo screen completely shield us. So wanting to share in Sophie's infectious happy mood, without time to think I pull my jeans down and unbutton my shirt.

Not quite as brave as Sophie I leave on my knickers and bra.

Picking my way gingerly over the mossy stones, I hold my breath and launch myself into the freezing water. Surprised at how the cold propels me, I breaststroke across the river to Sophie. It's so much fun. It must be a lovely memory for Sophie of Bella.

Splashing and laughing we race each other back to the bank.

The sun dips behind the trees as I pick my way over the rocks back up into the protection of the secret garden. Shivering, I pull on my dry clothes over soggy wet undies. Sophie more sensibly has dry clothes to pull on.

"Look, you have goose bumples." Sophie looks concerned.

"It's goosebumps, and yes I am freezing."

Sophie calls Biscuit, who is wetter than both of us, we jump out of the way as he shakes his coat sending droplets of water in all directions.

"Let's get you home and warmed up, I have some coq au vin in the slow cooker. We can 'ave an apéro and drink to Bella."

Almost too numb to reply, I let Sophie guide me back through the garden.

Reaching the garden door I remember the urn.

"What about the urn?" I say, turning my head in the direction of the river.

"It's past now, Izzy, we leave the urn here in the garden. Thank you for helping me to say goodbye. You need a hot deep bath," Sophie says as she unclips Biscuit's lead.

Nodding in agreement, it's been months since I have had a bath. There is just a tiny shower in my apartment above Le Petit Chat Noir, and Kim's gîte only had a wet room.

Sophie leads the way up the steps and narrow pathway that take us up to the room nestled into the side of the cliff. It's the only part of the house visible from the laneway. With its pink painted window I am curious to see what's inside, assuming these past months that it was a storeroom.

Pushing open the door we step inside. There is still just enough daylight for me to see a lovely old bath sitting in the middle of the room.

Sophie moves around the room lighting candles.

Shadows dance on the walls and through the window I can see across the river to the Palais de Justice. What a spellbinding room.

On the wall behind the bath a painting of Bella partly covered in a towel, her long red hair flowing over her breast. Reminding me again how much I look like my Aunt.

"Sorry there is no electricity in this room, we were—" Sophie stops herself. "I was, going to have it put on one day, but one day never comes. The hot water comes from the boiler downstairs, it takes a minute."

Sophie holds her hand under the running water.

"There you are, it's coming now."

I watch as Sophie takes a towel out of the old cupboard and places it across the wicker chair beside the bath. On top a cake of lavender soap.

"I will go and turn our dinner on," she says as she pulls the door quietly behind her.

My clothes have stuck to my wet underwear and I peel them away.

Stepping into hot water makes my skin tingle, and my muscles say thank you. Slowly slipping down till only my head is above the water.

In my own blissful world with my eyes closed thinking of today and all the days before it. Sensing movement, I open my eyes, Sophie is sitting on the chair beside the bath with the towel over her knees, standing up, she holds up the towel.

"Come on, my mermaid, our dinner is nearly ready."

I step out, holding onto the steep sides of the old bath. Sophie holds one side of the towel over my shoulders and using the other side dries my back. It seems so completely natural. She turns me around to face her enclosing me in the towel. "You're so like her," she says, touching my face.

166

Walking over to the cupboard she takes out a cotton dress and pale blue cardigan. "These were Bella's, they will fit you, I have been meaning to take them for the Red Cross shop."

Sophie's moment of tenderness to me passes, and she leaves me to dress.

My heart is fluttering, and I feel butterflies that I have never felt before.

Such a simple gesture to dry my back, so caring and gentle.

Sophie is right, I pull the pale blue dress over my head, and it sits perfectly on my waist, dropping just below my knees. My red curls reach just below the collar. My underwear is too wet to put on. The fabric is soft against my breasts and for the first time in my life I feel feminine.

Opening the door to the birds' evening song, I can smell the scent of coq au vin wafting up the pathway. Feeling starving, I walk carefully down the stairs, down the pathway opening the door into the kitchen. Sophie has her back to me and is busy at the cooker. All the candles are lit, and the room smells so delicious.

"Can I help?" I offer.

Sophie doesn't turn around but answers, "Yes, there is a bottle of champagne in the fridge, let's have an apéro."

The cork glides out effortlessly, and I set the bottle and two glasses on the trunk that doubles as a table. Sophie turns around when she hears the pop. She lets out a little gasp as she sees me. "You look beautiful, Izzy."

I am not used to compliments and can feel myself blushing.

Pouring the champagne, I don't reply.

Sophie slips her hand in mine and we stand together in the doorway, sipping our bubbles watching the last rays of the sun dip over the river.

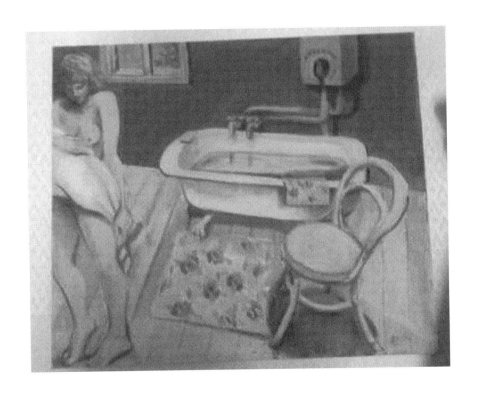

Painting by J Epstein 1982

Chapter 25

At first I wonder where I am, with eyes still closed I feel weight on my chest. Biscuit is stretched along beside me his face close to mine. His shiny brown eyes waiting patiently for me to wake. Stroking his head, I wriggle to make a space and pull myself up onto the pillows. Through the curtain canopy around the bed I can see Sophie and hear her humming.

The rich scent of coffee beans makes my butterflies growl with anticipation.

Through the shutters the early sun sends it's rays, warming my bare shoulders. Pulling the duvet around me smiling to myself, memories of the beautiful evening that was last night, fill my heart. Could it be possible to feel any happier?

Sophie breaks into my quiet reflection, handing me a mug of coffee. Pushing Biscuit to make a space, she curls up on the bed beside me, reaching over she gently tucks an escaping curl behind my ear. Neither of us mention last night, are we both too scared to believe that such tenderness and joy could be ours to keep?

My thoughts are dragged back to practicalities of the day.

Harriet's birth and death certificates have finally turned up at the Notaire's. Today I can finally make things right and sign the paperwork to complete the transfer of 32 Rue Puits Cornet to Sophie. I am busting to tell her but really want it to be a surprise. This Saturday is Kim's spring party, Sophie is coming and in front of our friends I am going to give her the deeds to the house. It will be a perfect celebration.

"Sorry, Sophie, I can't walk Biscuit this morning, I have some last minute things to fix for the shop." Pushing the duvet off I give her a hug. Not wanting her to think I expect anything after last night, I decide to go for friendly, not mushy, approach. Although my heart is bursting, a feeling that I have never experienced. Is it pain or pleasure? Just as

169

well I have important things to get done today and keep my feet on the ground, cause my head is so in the clouds.

I leave Bella's pretty dress on the end of the bed, pulling on my jeans. Biscuit jumps off the bed wagging his tail. "Sorry boy not today."

"Thanks for dinner, it was delicious," calling out to Sophie as I walk into the blue, blue happy day.

"Don't forget the party on Saturday."

"What time?" Sophie yells through the door.

Dragging open the green gate to the lane I can hardly wait for the weekend.

I shout back, "A vingt heures, 8pm, don't be late."

For the first time in my life, I am actually looking forward to a party.

Kim helped me choose an emerald green velvet dress, from her Alladin's cave cellar, racks and racks of gorgeous outfits collected from years of travelling.

When I looked at myself in her mirror I could not believe it was my reflection. It's been six months since I have stopped dying my hair and it's back to its original coppery red. Instead of Izzy from Park Orchards, I saw Isabella of Montmorillon, and felt like a queen from one of my favourite historical novels.

After years of sadness, Sophie deserves happiness, and the thought of our small group of friends there when I give her the deeds to the house, is just perfect. The only person that knows about my surprise is Hero, she is sworn to secrecy.

Cité de L'Ecrit, Montmorillon

Chapter 26

Usually the alarm wakes me, but this morning I have been awake since 5am. The sun slowly sending its rays into my sitting room and throwing a glow over tonight's dress hanging over the armoire at the end of my bed.

Six months ago, I was lost, too scared to dare dream of a different future, hugging my knees to my chest, I can feel my heart knows so much joy now. This stuff doesn't happen to me but my Wheel of Fortune has proved me wrong.

With just two weeks till the Salon du Livre and Le Petit Chat Noir opening, everything is in place downstairs. Today I will finish unpacking Bella's books from the attic and decide which novels to have on the shelves. Followed by a long walk and finish off the canapés for the party.

Still nothing back from Maria, but I haven't given up hope that she might make the opening. There is no phone line at the shop, so I will use the phone at Maisons Rurales office and try to call them next week.

The best part of living in the middle of the town is the scent of bread in the mornings and again in the evenings. With over twelve Boulangeries baking each day, making sure there is never a shortage of baguettes.

Today I need no encouragement to get out of bed. Get this day started.

Dressed in a scruffy old tracksuit and T-shirt I head around the corner to get croissants and a crusty nordic loaf for lunch. Waving to Jane and Kim, both already getting ready for today's Saturday trade. In just two weeks I will be a part of Vieux Pont shopkeepers.

Covered in dust, but satisfied with my morning's work, the last box is unpacked.

Trying to stay motivated this afternoon has been difficult. I keep thinking of the deeds rolled up ready for Sophie, sitting on my kitchen bench tied with a red velvet ribbon. Playing out in my mind my speech to thank everybody and especially Sophie for all her help and encouragement.

Flipping my head over and running my fingers through my messy curls, longer hair means lots of tangles. I work the anti-stat lotion through the way that the hairdresser Pasquale showed me. With more length and less frizz my hair sits all bouncy and shiny below my shoulders.

Stepping into the dress and pulling it up around my breasts it makes me feel almost regal. Finally I fasten the silver heart on a gold thread that Maria gave me for my 30th birthday. Planning to dance tonight with Sophie, I slip my feet into soft leather ballerina pumps.

La Terrasse is just two metres across the laneway from my shop. With canapés in one hand and the deeds rolled up in the other, I glance each way, hoping not to see anybody till I get into the safety of Kim's tearoom.

Kim has left the door unlatched for me, the wind chime rings softly as I step into the lush welcome of the cafe.

Kim looks up from the back of the tearoom, where she is hanging dried flowers. "Oh my God. Izzy you look so beautiful." I can feel myself blushing.

Not wanting to draw more attention to myself I return her compliment.

"It's your dress Kim, that's what's beautiful."

Watching Kim climb down the ladder in high heels, I hold my breath till she steps onto the safety of the carpet. She is wagging her finger at me,

"You stop it, Izzy, you take a compliment."

It's you that looks beautiful, look at your hair, it's stunning."

"All your hard work, all that exercise and healthy eating, you deserve a compliment."

Kim hugs me "Good on you."

"Thanks, Kim. It was all your encouragement," I add.

Starting to lay out the food on the tables while Kim finishes the decorations, I can feel nervous butterflies.

Bottles of bubbly and champagne glasses are all ready on the bar.

"Let the party begin." Kim pops the first cork.

Sounds of rockabilly change the tearoom into a jive bar.

I put the deeds for Sophie behind the bar, where nobody can spill anything on them. Glancing at my watch it's 8.20, and Sophie still hasn't arrived. Maybe I should have walked over with her, I know she is nervous about coming to parties with my friends.

Claude and Brigitte have arrived so Kim and I stand chatting to them.

James puts his arm around me. "Hello gorgeous, wow look at you."

"Excited about the shop opening?"

Glancing over James' shoulder through the crowd to the door in case I miss Sophie, I take a sip of my drink.

"Thanks, James, it looks like it's really going to happen, thanks for all your help."

"Blue Suede Shoes" blasts out, in a flash everybody is up dancing.

Just as I am starting to relax I hear a commotion near the entrance.

Through the crowded dance floor I see Sophie, oh, great she made it.

My joy turns to concern as I notice she is wobbly on her feet. As I get closer to her I can hear she is slurring her words. Yelling at Hero, her voice building to a scream.

She appears to be drunk.

I can't make any sense of it, she hardly ever has a drink.

"You knew, you knew," she repeats herself screaming at Hero.

"You all knew, she has just come to take my house!

I thought she loved me, but she has just come to take my house!"

My head is spinning, I can't believe what I am hearing.

"Where is she?" Sophie turns her rant to Kim.

Sophie continues at the top of her voice, "My friend saw her at the Notaire's yesterday, she thinks she can take my house."

"Well, you can all get fffff ucked."

Sophie turns, and stumbles out the front door, just as I get to Kim.

"Oh God, Kim, this is horrible. How could she get the wrong idea like this?" I gasp at Kim, shaking my head.

"Go after her, love, put it right, she's put two and two together and made five. Sometimes surprises are not such a good idea." Kim puts her hand on my arm.

"Go on find her, put it right," she urges me, nodding her head in the direction of the open door.

"I'll bring her back, it will be alright," I say, running towards the door.

Looking left towards the old town I step onto the cobblestones but my foot doesn't connect.

Screeching brakes, a horn. Turning towards the noise, I am flying like a butterfly, a mixture of pain and pleasure then black.

Le Vieux Pont, Montmorillon.

Chapter 27

Worms in my arm, and words my brain can't untangle. Trying to open my eyes sends blinding pain through my head. It's easier to retreat to my darkness.

Slowly the night seems less and less, and I am aware of a comforting touch on my fingers. Still so very tired I return to my cave.

Today my brain makes sense of a few words I hear floating in my head.

There is a soft murmuring around me, through the slits of my eyes I see shadows. Then they are gone and my comforting darkness pulls me back.

"Should we tell her?"

Tiny beams of sunlight are creeping through shuttered windows, a strong scent of honeysuckle. Struggling to focus, I can see heads in a very white room, where am I?

Words finally come to my lips and I mumble,

"Tell me what?"

"Oh mon Dieu. She is back with us."

Somebody rushes towards me, her long hair tumbles around my face, brown concerned eyes staring into mine.

She tries to hug me and I wince, the tubes in my arm, pulling. "Sophie," I say softly with all the strength I can muster.

"Where am I?"

"You were hit by a car, my Izzy. I thought you were dead.

It's all my fault, I am a stupid selfish old woman."

Big salty drops spill down her cheeks and drip onto my face.

"Sleep now, sleep, I am here, we are all here."

A white lady steps in and takes Sophie's arm she looks like an angel, I want to reach out to her but my arms are too heavy. More muttering and names are coming to faces. Kim, Hero, Patricia, giving a little smile is all I can do before I sink back into my healing sleep.

Days come and go but always when I wake Sophie is sitting in the chair beside my bed. Helping as the nurses allow her to feed and bathe me, only leaving my room for her own comfort stops.

Slowly my confusion passes, and although I cannot remember anything after arriving at Kim's party that night, I have recovered nearly all my previous memory.

The doctors say I am very, very lucky that my friends acted so quickly, calling the ambulance. Montmorillon Hospital being so close, just over the old bridge, probably saved my life. After surgery for a punctured lung, and a pin in my shoulder, they put me into an induced coma to allow the swelling in my brain to ease.

Today, I am sitting up on my own propped against the soft pillows, feeling anxious to restart my new life, outside of the hospital. Feeling the luckiest girl alive and thanking my angels.

When I moan about the hospital food and wanting to see Biscuit, and open Le Petit Chat Noir, Sophie chastises me: "Izzy, you not to hurry."

"Bon dans tous les temps," all in good time.

"'Allo, 'allo!" Brigitte pops her head around my screen.

My visitors have been restricted by the nurses and this is the first time in a month I have seen some of my old friends.

"Brigitte. So good to see you! My French words are coming slowly back but English is quicker.

"Merci pour le soupe," I say as she passes Sophie a blue and white dish, my taste buds can't wait, I miss my friend's cooking. Nurses and doctors are wonderful here, but the food is horrible. Seems even French hospitals have terrible food.

"It's your favourite oignon soupe," Brigitte nudges in beside Sophie, fighting for space on my bed.

Soon I will be home and can't wait to repay all this

kindness.

The doctors have agreed I may be able to leave by the end of the week.

My happiness is sapped when I see a look of concern pass between my friends.

"What's wrong?" I say, meeting their gaze.

"Well, there has been a little trouble at your shop," Sophie stutters, trying to find the right words in English.

"We didn't want to upsetting you."

Drawing myself up against the pillows, I get ready for what seems must be bad news.

I have no words, and sit waiting for the explanation. It's slow coming from Brigitte and Sophie. All sorts of thoughts are jumping into my head, and butterflies in my stomach are doing summersaults.

Now I wonder, why Kim, Jane and Pat have not been in visiting this week, and panic that something has happened to one of my dear friends.

"What's happened?"

"There was a vandal attack at your shop," Sophie blurts out, unable to keep it in any longer.

"What?"

"You know, a smashing and grabbing," Sophie tries to explain.

Brigitte puts her hand on mine and says, "These horrible people, they write the nasty words."

"What nasty words?" I am really at a loss as to what is going on or has happened and starting to lose my patience.

They both go quiet, a voice around the door says, "Lezzoes."

Kim cuts to the chase. "'Lesbians'. They painted the word right across your window love, sorry, but there is no easy way to say it."

"Narrow-minded nasty people."

Sophie looks crumpled, as though she personally was

responsible for what had happened.

"It's so horrible, Izzy, I didn't want to tell you," she whispers.

My heart starts to sink, all my joy of the past months washing down my face in a huge river of tears.

Kim passes me a tissue, then another and another, finally my sobs ease.

"Don't worry, love, this town cares about you, and we are all behind you and Sophie. The Gendarmes will find out who did this and it will be dealt with and finished."

It's all too much for me to take in, I hadn't realised that everybody has seen how my relationship with Sophie has been slowly moving from friendship to tenderness and caring that could possibly last a lifetime.

"I thought the town was accepting of what I was doing at the shop?" I direct my statement to Kim.

"Don't jump bridges, Izzy, it could be anybody. You have amazing support in this town and we can't wait for your Boutique to open."

"When did this happen? How long have I been kept in the dark?"

I'm starting to feel like a secret has been kept from me, and I am being treated like a child.

"Don't be angry with us, Izzy, we didn't want to upset you. We just didn't expect you to make such a quick recovery."

"It's all taken care of, a group of us have been working under the watchful eye of Pat and Keith, they have arranged for the façade to be redecorated," they all rush to tell me at once.

"It's nearly finished," Sophie beams at me.

Nurse Eveline makes an appearance, pretending to be cross with everybody, but giving a little smile,

"Everybody out, this girl needs her sleep, tomorrow she is being discharged."

Medieval Archangel, Montmorillon

Chapter 28

For the second time since I arrived in Montmorillon, I am being led across the Vieux Pont towards Le Petit Chat Noir.

This time I don't have my eyes closed, but instructed by Sophie to walk slowly, looking at the cobblestones so I don't lose my footing. My right arm is still in a sling and I am feeling slightly giddy from the fresh air and sunshine so very welcome after a month in my hospital room.

At Sophie's insistence, I have agreed to spend a few weeks recuperating at Rue Puits Cornet, but only if she will first let me see for myself the façade of my shop.

Since the news of the vandalism I can't get it out of my mind, my pretty home being damaged in that way.

Hearing a woof, I look up and Jane is holding Biscuit, who is desperately trying to break free and come to me. Behind her Pat and Keith are standing in their overalls, with Hero and Kim, everybody choruses:

"Welcome home, Izzy"

Le Petit Chat Noir looks just as I left it the day of my horrible accident, there is not a trace of vandalism, I know how hard they must have all worked to return it to its pretty facade.

One by one, everybody hugs and kisses me, my heart is bursting with gratitude and love, I can barely speak for the lump in my throat.

"Enough, enough." Sophie pretends to chastise them all.

"Time now for rest, come, Izzy, home to the sofa."

Sophie takes my good arm and we walk slowly over the bridge, down Rue Puits Cornet. Jane follows behind with Biscuit, afraid he will knock me over with his happiness.

Settled on the sofa at Sophie's I can feel myself drifting into a welcome doze, this is the most I have done in over a month, and I feel completely exhausted. Tomorrow I will start to make plans again for the shop's opening. The Salon du Livre has come and gone but there is still a few months of the busy summer and autumn to come. Sophie takes the cup and saucer from me before I drop them. It's heaven to be home and I am the luckiest girl alive.

Le Vieux Pont,

the old bridge leading to Cité de L'Ecrit, Montmorillon, France.

Chapter 29

Waking to the sun slipping over the duvet cover takes my mind back to our first night together. Is it possible that was only just over a month ago? It seems an age ago, another life. Perhaps surviving such a near death situation is making me feel I have been reborn. My Tower of the cards nearly took my chance away, but the Wheel of Fortune has given it back to me.

Scratching at the door, and a howl, turn my attention in the direction of the kitchen. Sophie has locked Biscuit out to stop him jumping onto the bed and re-injuring my arm.

"Mon petit chien," she coos to Biscuit; trying to calm him: "Bientôt bientôt, soon you can come in." I love the way the way her French is so musical, even in her just-woken dishevelled state, she is so beautiful to watch, tumbling hair over her pretty elfin face.

A surge of warmth rushes through me, I want to stay here with Sophie, but she has said nothing of our night together since my accident. Her tenderness and caring speaks volumes to me, but being old fashioned I need to hear her say in her own words that she wants us to be together. Pushing it to the back of my mind, I try to focus on getting better and following my dream of Le Petit Chat Noir.

As Sophie makes the coffee she turns chatting to me.

"This morning we have visitors, Capitaine Girand from the Gendarmerie and James."

This takes me by surprise, and I wonder if it's just a friendly visit, or the Gendarmes have some news about the vandalism to my shop?

Sophie continues without pause. "So, they are arriving at 11am, that gives us two hours to get you dressed and tidy up."

"Do you know why they are coming, Sophie?"

"James called me last night, after you fell asleep, saying the

189

Gendarmes had some news for you, we will have to wait and see."

Sophie leaves me to dress slowly, while she takes Biscuit for a walk to the patisserie, all sorts of thoughts are buzzing through my head.

With Biscuit happily left running in the garden, Sophie has returned with *tarte citron* and *éclair chocolat*, the kitchen smells amazing. The rich smell of coffee dripping into the pot seems to summon the doorbell.

"Bonjour." James pops his head around the half-open kitchen door, closely followed by Capitaine Girond. Sophie jumps up to pull open the door, I stay seated on the sofa looking apprehensive.

"Bonjour, ça va?" She greets them both warmly, James walks over and plants a kiss on each of my cheeks.

Capitaine Gironde is more formal, but smiling, and I relax thinking it must be good news.

After shaking my left hand, he perches on the chair opposite me, Sophie has popped a faded cushion on to cover the broken wicker.

James and Sophie sit either side of me on the sofa and we all tuck into the delicious treats from the patisserie.

Wiping the crumbs from his chin, Capitaine Gironde leans slightly forward on his chair,

"Well, Madame Izzy, we have good news today for you." he looks around to make sure we are all paying attention. I can hardly breathe.

"The person, or persons that caused the damage to your shop were very foolish." I nod my head urging him to continue.

"In the laneway across from your shop they left behind some evidence, a can of spray paint," he exclaims, looking satisfied with himself.

"This has been safely delivered to the forensic department in Poitiers."

I feel as though I am in a page of an Agatha Christie novel, and just wish he would spit it out. Capitaine Gironde is enjoying the suspense.

"Yesterday they called my office, and the fingerprints have been matched with somebody known to us."

"Yes. Whooo?" Sophie and James are as impatient as me.

Capitaine Gironde is determined to enjoy every last second of his glory, and taking a deep breath he says,

"The fingerprints belong to Monsieur Jean-Claude Allardet."

I feel a rush of disgust at the mention of his name, and the memory of the day he tried to assault me. To think I had been prepared to forgive, and say he needed help.

"But I thought he was living in Limoges?" I stammer.

"He has been seen around Montmorillon these past weeks, and it seems he was still very angry." Capitaine Gironde glances at his watch and realises it is nearly midday, time for lunch. Standing up he concludes far more quickly.

"You have nothing to worry about, Izzy, he has been arrested, and taken in for questioning. We have enough evidence to convict him, he has been an embarrassment for the town. He will receive rehabilitation as part of his sentence."

James walks towards the door, following the Capitaine.

"Well; Izzy, fantastic news, Jean Claude will get the help he needs and you can relax about your shop." James pats me on the back.

"Start planning that opening party."

Chapter 30

Today, finally the all clear came from Doctor DuPont and my arm is out of the sling. It's been another three weeks of frustration at not being able to do things when and where I want, mixed with the joy of having Sophie fuss over me.

Sophie can finally get back to her painting, and I can focus on the final arrangements for next Saturday's opening of Le Petit Chat Noir.

The opening will be 10am, officiated by the president of the Montmorillon Commerce Committee, and champers for everybody.

In the afternoon we are having canapés made by Sophie, Kim is baking her famous carrot cake and caramel slice. James has helped me to put up posters and print little leaflets which we have left all over town. Sophie even drove me to some of the surrounding villages to put information in all the little bars.

Brigitte and Claude have a big sign in their supermarché window, everybody is invited to a party on Saturday night, on Kim's Terrasse after the closing of my first day of trade.

Many of our friends in Monty are musicians so have all agreed to bring instruments along to the party. Now all I need is for the universe to provide us with a beautiful Montmorillon balmy evening.

With my head full of party thoughts I don't even see Sophie standing in the doorway.

Stepping over the flagstone and into the shop she walks towards me holding out an envelope.

"This arrived today, I thought it might be urgent?" Concern is etched on her face. Looking at the envelope I instantly recognise Maria's handwriting.

My heart skips a beat and my butterflies twirl.

Sophie puts her hand on my back as if to steady me. Ripping open the envelope, one tiny page flutters to the ground, I scoop it up.

Park Orchards
Melbourne, Victoria
Australia

My Dearest Isabella,
We are so, so happy to be finally coming to be with you, forgive this surprise arranged by your friend Kim. We land at Limoges Airport, midday on Saturday 19th July. She's arranged already for our collection. We can't wait to hug you our Bella

Love Maria and Joe xx

I can barely read the words out loud, my joy catches in my throat. "Oh Sophie, they're coming, they're coming."

Hugging Sophie, I pick her up and squeal like a child.

Putting her down, I go racing out the door and across the cobblestones to Kim's, pushing her doorbell impatiently as it's not opening hours till midday.

Kim pushes back the curtain on the door and quickly unlocks the shutter.

"What's all the noise about?" she laughs.

"How long have you known Maria was coming? I am speaking so fast my words are a babble.

"I phoned her when you came out of hospital, we wanted it to be a surprise, but you know how sometimes surprises go wrong?"

We both laugh together,

"Hero and I decided it was enough of a surprise for you to find out a few days before they arrive."

"Thank you, thank you," I shout, running back to Sophie.

Sophie is still standing patiently, in the shop, with a smile on her face.

As I step over the flagstone she says, "I have one more surprise for you, Izzy. Last week, I sold one of the paintings of Bella. Madame Dupont paid 1000 euros, she wants the painting for her foyer. I want to use the money to take us on a holiday to Vietnam. I want you to meet my dear friends there, they run a little guest house in Quy Nhon. Will you come with me, Izzy? On a little holiday?"

I think I am going to explode, finally Sophie is asking me in her way, to be a part of her life. To meet her friends.

For the second time that day, I pick up Sophie and twirl her around.

"Of course, I would love to meet your friends. But, it will have to be after the summer here, in Monty."

"Trust me," Sophie says, "after the busy summer here we will both need a holiday."

After the excitement of the morning, it's hard to calm myself down. Trying to get back to the finishing touches of the window display, all the time thinking of my angels, Dad, and Aunt Bella who seems to have cast her spell, drawing me to Montmorillon. I wish that Harriet could see how different my new life is and how happy I am.

Kim has arranged for Maria and Joe to stay in her gîte. It's perfect that they will be staying where I first started my Montmorillon journey. They will be just across the road from the shop, and just around the corner from Sophie's at Rue Puits Cornet.

Planning to stay for three weeks, just long enough for us to show them everything that makes Montmorillon so special. I so want them to love it here and return again and again.

Stepping outside, I sit on the road outside Le Petit Chat Noir, the window looks just perfect. Tiny angels and butterflies dancing on their ribbons, medieval tarot cards, sparkling crystals, books full of magical history, eroticism and esoterics. Lilac curtains match the shutters and give just enough cover to make people inquisitive about what's inside. Shelves lined with runes nestled into crushed velvet lining, soft chairs that my clients can sink into while they wait to have their reading.

Happy I can do no more, I pick myself up and walk over the bridge to Sophie for our last evening together before the biggest day of my life and the opening of Le Petit Chat Noir.

Pausing halfway across the Vieux Pont, stepping up onto the pathway, leaning, touching the cool stone wall, my gaze takes in the majestic Gartempe River, winding its way through Montmorillon and on through the beautiful Vienne, it still takes my breath away. Thank you, Bella, I say quietly and blow her a little kiss.

Le Petit Chat Noir.

Chapter 31

"Merci merci, à bientôt." The crystal wind chime clinks softly as I close the door behind the last customers of the day.

Walking back into the middle of Le Petit Chat Noir I flop into the deep velvet cushions and let them soothe my weary body. What a day this has been.

The shelves are looking half empty and my group for the first tarot classes is full. Thank goodness, I have more pretty tarot and angel cards just waiting for their place on the shelves.

A constant stream of friendly faces has filled my first afternoon in the shop, many with little bunches of lily of the valley to wish me good luck.

Claude, Brigitte and all their French friends.

My poor muscles are crying out for a bath, that will have to wait till my next sleepover at Sophie's. For now, I run up the stairs to have a quick shower and get ready for tonight's party.

Deliberately I don't turn on the hot water, letting the cold water run in streams down my back and between my breasts. It's heavenly and revives me, citron soap from Sophie leaves my skin tingling.

Months ago, Jane helped me choose some beautiful cotton fabric from Le Petite Mercerie. She has made it into an elegant Chinese dress for me. It's the first time I have ever had anything made to measure. Pulling up the clever hidden zip, the top fits perfectly around my chest. Flaring out gently at my waist, white silk trousers sit snugly underneath.

Turquoise, rose and lilac birds of paradise nestled into blue and green petit flowers, the fabric is so joyful. I feel *très exotique*. Slipping into jade green ballet slippers that will be perfect for dancing, ready as I am going to be, I skip down the stairs two by two.

Kim insisted on taking Maria and Joe straight to the gîte to rest, I am bursting to see them and wonder what Maria will think of my new-found confidence.

Looking at my watch it's already 8pm, no time for a fancy hairdo. Tipping my head forward and running my fingers through this tangly mess will have to do.

As I close the door behind me the sounds of the double bass and saxophone float gently up La Terrasse lane. I decide to slip in the back way without going through the tearoom.

Walking up steps and pushing open the gate, I am met by a scene that takes my breath away. Tiny fairy lights twinkling along the grapevine, coloured lanterns swinging in the soft evening breeze. Candles on the tables sending dancing fairy shadows over the stone walls.

Overlooking the river, Kim and Hero are perched on the stone wall, chatting to Sophie, glasses of bubbly in hand, everybody looks so happy. Taking a deep breath I walk slowly towards them, one by one they look up, smiling, calling to me.

Sophie joins me, slipping her hand into mine, she whispers, "You are beautiful." My butterflies flutter, my heart swells as I give her hand a little squeeze.

"Bella, Bella!" Behind me a voice rings out that I have not heard for such a long time.

Turning from Sophie's embrace I see my beautiful Maria running towards me. Gulping back sobs I run into her ample bosom. She hugs me so tightly, I can't breathe, then pushing me back, she looks at me through happy tears. Neither of us speaks. Joe walks quietly behind, pulling me into a gentle hug.

"This is the first time I have seen Maria lost for words," he laughs.

With Sophie holding one hand and Maria the other, we look out over the sparkling Gartempe river to the majestic Notre Dame, beautiful in her evening splendour.

Gently, I take Sophie's other hand and pull her around so she is facing Maria. Joe is already off jiving with Hero.

"Maria, this is Sophie, my love," I say tenderly squeezing Sophie's hand.

Maria's smile couldn't be bigger, "Oh, Izzy, I am so happy, happy, for you," she says through joyful tears.

The Notre Dame bells ring out, competing with the saxophone.

Kim hands me a glass of bubbles. "You did it, Izzy, congratulations, let's PARTY!"

My Wheel of Fortune has lifted me up, good luck and happy butterflies are mine. Looking around encircled by beautiful friends, Sophie's hand in mine, I couldn't be happier.

None of us can stay the same, we have to evolve and let our spirits soar. I don't know what the future holds, but for this moment in time, Magical Montmorillon is my world.

Sweet dreams Aunt Bella.

The World.

Rider-Waite Tarot deck.

About the Author

Rosie Christopherson grew up in suburban Melbourne, Australia. After travelling and running a guest house in Vietnam with her partner Huw, they now live in a rambly 17th century house on the banks of the Gartempe River in Montmorillon, France.

Rosie has a diploma in esoteric studies.

Bonne Chance and Butterflies is her first novel.

45068153R00120

Printed in Poland
by Amazon Fulfillment
Poland Sp. z o.o., Wrocław